I0653884

Some Like It Fox

MARY FRAME

Copyright © 2023 by Mary Frame

All rights reserved.

No part of this publication may be reproduced, distributed, or transmitted in any form or by any means, including photocopying, recording, or other electronic or mechanical methods, without the prior written permission of the publisher, except as permitted by U.S. copyright law. For permission requests, contact Mary Frame maryframeauthor@gmail.com

The story, all names, characters, and incidents portrayed in this production are fictitious. No identification with actual persons (living or deceased), places, buildings, and products is intended or should be inferred.

Book Cover by Qamber Designs

https://www.qamberdesignsmedia.com/

Content edits by Catherine Felnagle

Copy edits by Elizabeth Nover at Razor Sharp Editing

www.razorsharpediting.com

For my grandparents, Don and Pauline Humphrey, who were the embodiment of genuine love and two of the best humans to ever exist <3

Preface

Dear reader,

This book contains references to past deaths of parents and young sibling by illness or accident. There is also a character struggling with past alcohol abuse and addiction.

Thematically, this entire series is a little more heart-wrenching than my other books, but there still is humor —because life is messy, but it's also funny.

I provide this warning so you can make an informed decision about whether or not to proceed. If you would rather read something more lighthearted, please check out the Imperfect series or The Dorky series if you haven't already!

Take care of yourself,
    <3 Mary

CHAPTER
One

I turn the key in the ignition for the seventh time, as if by some miracle *this time* will be different than the past six.

The engine sputters, giving me a half-hearted cough before wheezing into dead silence.

"Please work," I mutter into my steering wheel. "Please, please, please, don't do this to me." The mantra of anyone who's ever had their vehicle crap out in the middle of a freaking blizzard at night.

I'm less than ten miles from my family home. The road in front of me is blanketed in white, the flakes winging through the night air like I've been plunked down in the center of a snow globe and shaken up.

Ten miles. So close, and yet way too far to try and trek the rest of the way on foot.

I should have stopped for gas an hour ago, but I thought I could make it.

Killing the headlights, I slip from the driver's seat into the back of the VW bus, grabbing my bag from the sink and pawing through it for my cell. The screen is black. Dead.

It's an old phone, the charge never lasts long, and I am eternally forgetting to plug it in. I like to use my old iPod to listen to music when I'm on the road because I don't have to worry about music cutting out when I'm driving through the backwoods, or if a call comes in. Plus, without music playing, I lose my ever-loving mind.

Of course, now, I may be losing my ever-loving life.

Staring blankly out the darkened window, I consider my options.

There are houses spread out along this route. Ranch-style homes with lots of surrounding property. Bonus, I grew up in this town, so I know most of the residents.

It's the night before Christmas Eve. Someone has to be home. I just don't know how far away the nearest house is since the windows reveal nothing more than squares of black flashing with snow.

I could hunker down, sleep here, possibly die of hypothermia.

Or venture out in the storm, possibly die sooner.

At least my family won't be worried. They also won't be coming to the rescue.

Last week I told Finley I couldn't make it until tomorrow, and I meant it at the time. I didn't want to spend more hours than absolutely necessary with Mindy.

The thought of spending even a minute in the same room makes me want to jump out of my own skin.

At the moment, I have more pressing things than my sister feud to concern myself with, like dehydration. I have maybe half a liter of water, no heat, and a box of expired Froot Loops in the cupboard.

Think, Taylor, think.

I stare blankly out the window. A light glints, flickering through the driving snow.

There.

Is that a porch light?

It disappears a second later as the snow increases in intensity, blocking it from view.

I blink. Am I imagining things?

I've been stranded for five minutes, and I'm already hallucinating.

I sit up, moving closer to the window, eyes straining through the thick flakes dumping outside.

There is it again.

My heart lifts. That is definitely a light. There is no question about it. It has to be a porch light. It might be the Petersons' place. Paul worked with Dad sometimes around our family property. He's a brawny guy, well over six feet tall, and barely speaks. His wife, Moira, was the school nurse when I was in elementary school. She was tiny, half his size, and a ball of fire. They also had two girls, both almost ten years younger than me.

Or maybe it's Delilah Gardner's place. She retired

from city hall years ago. It could be the Minellis'. Their son was a couple of years ahead of me at Whitby High.

Whoever it is, someone must be home. I have to try it.

If no one's home, I'll come straight back to the bus and bunker down.

Please, someone be home.

I pull on thermal pants and a long-sleeve shirt, covering them with thick sweats, a sweater, and my coat. Wind blasts, shaking the van and nearly knocking me on my ass.

Okay then.

I remove the outerwear and sweats, add another layer of clothes over my thermals, then cover it all up again. I step into my best waterproof boots, grab my overnight bag, and head into the storm.

The icy wind sucks the breath from my lungs. Pinpricks of freezing snowflakes pelt me in the face, stinging my skin. I duck my head under the hood of my coat and trudge in the direction of the light, glancing up periodically to make sure I don't go off course.

Halfway there, my eyes locked on the glowing bulb ahead, it winks out, as if smothered by the surrounding blackness.

A gasp flies out of my throat, creating a misty cloud of air in front of my face. I halt in my tracks.

I glance behind me, the bus obscured by the flying snow.

Keep going. I push ahead, forging through snow-drifts. This is taking forever. I must be off course.

Out of nowhere, the porch appears in front of me, as if it just erupted from the earth.

I stomp up the wooden steps and bang on the bright blue door with a gloved fist. This must be the Petersons' place. I remember the colorful door. I came here with Dad once when he needed to borrow some kind of tool or something. I must have been a freshman in high school.

The covered porch blocks out some of the wind. I shove the hood off my head and glance around.

Only the sound of my breathing breaks the stillness. The windows are dark and silent.

Maybe no one is home. Maybe they went somewhere for the holidays. But I swear that light was on.

I glance behind me, into the night beyond. It's only around seven, but the sky is as oppressive as the dark side of midnight.

Making my way over to the window by the front door, I peer inside. My heart leaps at the flickering light behind the curtain. What is that? A fireplace?

My stomach rumbles, an audible reminder that I haven't eaten since breakfast.

The door swings open and I spin toward the sound.

I look up. And up. Every cell in my body stands to full attention.

A hulking man looms in the doorway, holding a pillar candle in one hand. The gentle light glances over his glossy dark hair and highlights his prominent, high-bridged nose and a square jaw lined with stubble. The shape of his mouth is full with pouty lips, a contrast to the sharp angles of his jaw.

A gust of wind blows past us, into the house, knocking out the flickering candle in his hand.

"Come on in." He steps back, motioning for me to enter.

I follow him inside.

He shuts the door and I tense.

What am I doing? I walked right into some strange man's home without a second thought.

"The power went out." His voice is a deep rumble that vibrates down to my toes.

"I can see that."

We stare at each other, him still holding the unlit candle, me clutching my bag strap like it's a weapon.

Who is this guy? He doesn't ask why I've appeared on his doorstep in the middle of the storm of the century, like the ghost of Christmas past.

What if he's a serial killer? What if he broke in and the Petersons are tied up in the basement? My fingers are gripping my bag so hard my fingers ache. I have pepper spray. Is it in the main pouch or the side pocket?

I swallow and shift on my feet, my gaze darting to the door behind him. "Um. Are you related to the Petersons? This is their house, right? Do they still live here? Are they around somewhere?" My heart pounds in my ears, my palms sweaty in my gloves. The fireplace illuminates the room, and I absorb the details in flashes, taking in a beige couch, a dark wood coffee table, and Tiffany lamps on the end tables.

"Moira is my aunt. This is their house. They still live here, but they're out of town for the holidays."

The words break through the looming panic, bringing with them a fuzzy piece of knowledge.

That's right. They had a nephew who moved in with them during high school.

Wow. The recovered memory bursts over the surface of my mind, sending chills up my spine. How had I forgotten? I reach for his name in my mind, but it escapes me.

He moved to Whitby in the middle of our junior year. The same year everything changed. I went from honors student to barely managing to squeak through my senior year, aided by teachers with pitying eyes.

High school ceases to be important when your little sister dies.

The grip on my bag relaxes an inch. I know him. He's not a murderer. Then it comes rushing back to me.

"Wait." My mouth pops open. "Atticus?"

His eyes widen. "You remember?"

"Of course I remember." Some, anyway. He was always quiet, always off to the side, like a shadow in the corners of my already dim memories.

The Atticus of my youth looks nothing like the rugged Adonis standing in front of me. He was tall when we were in high school, but he was so gangly then. His eyes are the same, warm brown with caramel highlights. His hair was longer and eternally draped over his face, like he was trying to hide himself from the world. It's shorter now, but still long enough for the disheveled strands to tickle his neck.

"I'm Taylor Fox," I say automatically, still weaving through forgotten recollections from high school. Something shimmers in the back of my mind, an image flashing to the forefront. Atticus's hands on a steering wheel while afternoon sunshine pours through the windows, warming the cab of a truck. *What is that?*

"I know." He sets the candle on a table by the door, then opens a drawer, fumbling inside. He pulls out a flashlight, clicks it on, and hands it to me. Then he uses a lighter to relight his candle, before putting it back in the drawer.

I unlatch my fingers from my bag strap, happy for the heavy weight of the flashlight in my hand.

"You can put your things down wherever you like." He motions to the chair on my left.

After a second's hesitation, I put my bag down and then shrug out of my coat.

He takes it from me, draping it over the back of the chair.

My stomach growls, loud enough to fill the quiet space and cover the crackle of the fireplace.

He frowns.

I wince, my face heating. "Sorry."

Without a word, he stalks past me, a whiff of fresh soap mixed with a trace of cedar cologne breezing by. He smells good. Clean. I probably smell like stomped ass since I've been driving stressed for hours. At least I showered this morning.

I lift the flashlight and follow, the beam tracing over his gray Henley. The shirt is just tight enough to highlight the broadness of his back. The light trails down to his tapered waist, illuminating the jeans hugging his ass.

Wowza.

Awareness rushes through me, and I force the flashlight up.

Do not ogle Atticus.

I should be too exhausted to be turned on. I've barely slept over the past week of traveling, prior to which I was at the Beale Street Music Festival in Tennessee.

My gaze slips down again.

Don't think about his ass.

An impossible feat when it's just there, taunting me.

I clear my throat. "I'm so sorry to barge in on you like this, on the night before Christmas Eve and all."

He passes through an open archway leading into a country-style kitchen. I shine the flashlight around, taking in the white cabinets, butcher block counters, and copper sink.

He sets his candle down on the island, casting a gentle glow on the surface, then opens a cupboard, pulling out a loaf of bread and a jar of peanut butter. He lifts his brows at me. "Peanut butter and jelly okay?"

My stomach groans in anticipation. I would eat cat food right now. "That sounds perfect."

"How many?"

I shrug. "A million."

The corner of his mouth twitches.

"Two would be great."

I set the flashlight on the counter, pointing it in his general direction to offer additional illumination without blinding him.

He opens the fridge, grabbing a jar of jelly.

I hop into one of the upholstered chairs next to the island. "My bus ran out of gas, and I saw the porch light and I didn't know what else to do because my phone is dead. Do you have a phone I could borrow? I should call my family."

He stops midspread with the butter knife, setting it to the side before retrieving a sleek black phone out of his back pocket, unlocking it, and sliding it over to me.

"Thanks." I stare down at the screen. I'll call them after I eat. I nibble my bottom lip. Or maybe I won't. I don't want them to worry.

I push the phone to the side. "Where are Paul and Moira? And your cousins?"

"They're out of town."

I frown. "Without you?"

The knife stills over the open jar of peanut butter. "I had work through yesterday. They don't know I'm here. I didn't know I would be able to make it home in time for the holidays until the last minute." He shrugs, giant shoulders shifting up and down. "I'm only here for a few days anyway. They went to Bermuda."

"Where do you work?"

"I'm a field botanist. I sort of work everywhere. Anywhere they need me."

"Oh." I'm not sure exactly what that means, but before I can ask, he turns around, handing me a plate with the double stack of sandwiches.

All thoughts go flying out the window, my attention turning to filling the gaping hole in my stomach.

I take a giant bite and suppress the urge to groan. It's probably because I'm starving, but this is the best thing I've ever tasted.

Once I've wolfed down the first sandwich, I come up for air. "I didn't think I would make it home today either. My family doesn't even know I'm here. Not because I was working or anything, but because—I travel a lot," I finish lamely. Because I only work on a needs-must basis, and usually at some random dive bar or restaurant to make quick cash for gas, necessities, and to cover the cost of traveling to various music festivals around the country. Last year, I also put some extra funds into hiring a private investigator, which meant I had to work a little more than usual, but it will be worth it.

I hope.

I stuff sandwich number two into my mouth while he puts away the foodstuffs.

"Water?"

I nod, mouth full, and he grabs a bottle from the fridge and sets it in front of me.

When he leans back, the glow from the candle glints on a silver chain around his neck, disappearing under the neckline of his shirt.

I stop chewing, a memory rushing over me.

That necklace. I know what's at the end of that chain, concealed by fabric.

I stared at it, one sunny afternoon while Atticus drove me home from school, shortly after Aria died.

My entire world had been shattered into smithereens. I couldn't eat. I couldn't sleep. Every waking moment was like breathing in wet concrete.

During lunch, I would hide in the library because I didn't want to interact with anyone. Death is awkward. Most people don't know how to respond in the face of such senseless tragedy. Some offered uneasy sympathy, others pretended nothing had happened, while a bunch of my so-called friends gave me a wide berth.

One day, Atticus found me in the recesses of the library, hiding in the back of the stacks.

"Do you need a ride home?"

I nodded and then followed him out without a word.

The entire drive, I sat in the passenger seat, my gaze continually drawn to his profile.

After a few minutes of staring, he tossed me a glance before his eyes focused back on the road and a flush crept up his neck and into his cheeks.

"I like your necklace." I could only make out the edge of it in profile. The sun streaming through his windshield made the thin silver chain sparkle against his skin. I'd seen the pendant before, when we'd crossed paths in school, and earlier when he'd found me in the library. It was a tree, the branches sprawling and twisting out from the trunk, reaching for the edges of the smooth circle surrounding it.

"My mom gave it to me."

There were whispers when he first moved to town. His parents had died, and he'd been sent to live with his aunt and uncle.

So he knew.

We drove in silence, until curiosity poked at me. "What does the tree mean?"

"It's the tree of life. It represents a force that connects us all, through life and death."

Life and death. Two sides of the same coin. One is not possible without the other, a fact I'd been confronted with when we buried my baby sister.

"It's beautiful." The word cracked in my mouth. I averted my gaze from his profile, staring out the window, swallowing back the heaviness that threatened to consume me at any given moment.

Sometime later, he pulled off the main road and onto the gravel drive. I directed him through the Fox Cottages property and up to the house.

I paused, fingers on the door handle. "Does it ever get better?"

"No." The word was soft, quiet, apologetic.

I pushed open the door. Before I could shut it behind me, Atticus spoke again.

"She'll always be gone."

And isn't that the worst part? *Always* is too interminable to fathom. I'll never hear her laugh again. I'll never braid her hair, tease her about her crooked smile, or be there when she falls in love and has her heart broken. She won't experience any of it, cut from life too soon.

"Eventually, though, you'll be able to breathe."

"When?"

"I . . . I don't know. It takes as long as it takes."

Without another word, I shut the car door, and I never looked back.

The entire interaction became lost to the black fog that encompassed those months.

"Did you want anything else?" Atticus's voice yanks me back to the present. "I think we have some stale pretzels somewhere." He leans back against the counter, arms crossing over his chest.

The forgotten memories of a kind boy only add to his current brawny appeal. I drink in the broadness of his chest, the way his figure tapers down to his waist, and how his thighs fill his jeans.

Do I want anything else?

Why yes, I think I do. It's been a long time since I've been with anyone. Way too long since I experienced this level of attraction. Atticus is beyond tempting.

I tap on the water bottle. "Do you have anything stronger to drink?"

CHAPTER
Two

If someone had told me yesterday that I would be sitting on my couch, sharing a nightcap with Taylor Fox in front of a crackling fire, I would have laughed in their face.

And yet, here we are, chatting like we're old friends.

"So why did you have work so close to the holidays?" She sips bourbon from the tulip glass nestled in her hand and tucks her legs underneath her, angling her body in my direction.

We're sitting on opposite ends of the couch, only a couple of feet apart.

I swirl my own glass in my hand. "I do botanical surveys and environmental inspections for utility and construction companies. It's a lot of travel."

"You get paid to travel?" She rubs her lips together, the plump bit of skin glossy from her drink.

I nod and try not to stare, try not to imagine what the bourbon tastes like on her lips.

"That sounds incredible."

I rub the back of my neck. "The work is great, but constantly being on the road is not so great."

Her head tilts to one side. "You don't like it?"

I take a sip of my drink, considering how to answer the question without sounding ungrateful. "I've been working almost nonstop since graduation. I love being outside, and the work itself is fulfilling, but I don't know. I guess I feel like even though I'm constantly on the move and seeing new places it's like I'm missing out on something."

Like this holiday trip. My family went to Bermuda, and I'm here alone. It's no one's fault except mine. They wanted me to join them, but I told them to go on without me.

She chuckles. "I'm the opposite. It's like if I'm not out somewhere, actively moving and on the go, I'm missing out on everything. The FOMO is real." She pulls her hair off to one side with her free hand. The strands are dark and shiny, flowing in waves down to the middle of her back.

I clear my throat and try to clear my mind of thoughts of Taylor's hair spread across my pillowcase. "Where do you go?"

She takes another sip of her drink and then stares down at the glass in her lap. "I travel all over the country and go to music festivals and events and things like that. I don't get paid to do it, but it makes me happy."

Before I can make a comment, she keeps going, her eyes downcast, her fingers fiddling with the edge of her sweater. "It can be an uncomfortable conversation at parties or weddings." She pitches her voice higher, "What do you do? Oh, I live like a vagabond, party a lot, and have no idea what it means to have a 401k or gainful employment in general." She laughs, but the sound is brittle.

My hand clenches in my lap. A person shouldn't be defined by what they do, but by how they treat people. Even when I was the new kid who was too tall and too quiet and too weird, Taylor was always kind. She would wave to me in the hall and chitchat when we were in line at the cafeteria, and she smacked Jonathan Leland in the back of the head when he teased me for being a beanpole.

The crush was massive.

I lift my glass to her. "It takes courage to do what makes you happy, despite other people's expectations."

Her mouth spreads in a slow smile. "Thank you." Her eyes flicker over me before darting away.

Was she checking me out?

I shift in my seat, swallowing hard. *Pull it together.* "How did you get into it, all the traveling and festivals?"

"I went to Bonnaroo after high school with some friends and it changed my life." Her smile falters. "I needed to get away from Whitby and it was the perfect escape."

I'll never forget that day in the library after Aria died. Taylor was huddled in a ball in the farthest corner, her face devoid of any of the radiance that normally animated her features.

For me, Whitby was a refuge from my mourning.

For Taylor, it's a reminder of everything she lost.

She's regained some of that glow, but the darkness is still there, muted now, but present all the same. Grief isn't something that you leave behind, it's something you learn to live with.

"I've never been to a music festival."

Her eyes widen and she leans forward. "What? Seriously, you have to go."

"You'll have to give me tips. Let me know which ones are the best for a first-timer." I angle in her direction.

"Absolutely. Oh!" She reaches out with her free hand, grabbing my arm. "You have to go to Electric Forest, it is incredible. It's so much more than a music festival. The lights are amazing, the art is fantastic, it's like exploring another world. But the best part is the vibes. Everyone is so lovely, and they take care of each other, it's like you're suddenly family with strangers."

She doesn't move back, her hand still on my arm.

I look down at where she's touching me, and then our eyes lock.

Electric heat crackles around us. Lust shoots up my

spine and spreads through my limbs, coating my body with a lazy warmth.

She swallows and pulls away, taking a larger sip of the drink in her hands.

I take my own hefty gulp. Is this a one-sided attraction? The aftereffects of my childhood crush painting the situation in bold strokes?

I clear my throat. "Do you miss your family when you're gone?"

She sets her drink on the side table, the flickering candle beside it glinting light off the glass. "I come home a lot to visit. They're . . . mostly supportive of my lifestyle."

"Mostly?"

Her soft laughter curls through me. "They tease me all the time."

"Why would they tease you?"

She waves a hand. "I know, right? I'm the Empress of Awesome. Of course Jake likes to call me the Overlord of Lame."

I huff out a laugh. "How is Jake? What has he been up to?" I didn't talk to Jake much in school since he's a year younger than Taylor and me, but Whitby High was fairly small as far as high schools go. There were only about a hundred people in our graduating class.

"He works at Camp Aria with Finley."

My brows lift. "Camp Aria? No more Fox Cottages, or is it an addition to the rental properties?" The Fox family has owned a bunch of short-term rental cabins right outside town for as long as I can remember. I haven't spent much time back in town over the past few years, and Paul and Moira don't share local gossip. Before my cousins went to college, they were always the ones who kept me apprised of the local gossip.

She shakes her head. "Nope, not an addition. Fox Cottages has been no more since last year."

"How did that happen?"

She blows out a breath. "It's kind of a long story."

I motion to the dim room. "I've got time."

The corner of her mouth quirks up. "Finley took over the property after Dad passed. She and Jake managed it by themselves for a while, but it wasn't sustainable. The cabins were old and falling apart and basically bleeding money. Then, this big-time investor wanted to buy it. Oliver Nichols, have you heard of him?"

"No."

"He's actually dating Piper now, which is a whole different story, but anyway, he started pestering Finley to sell and buying up all the properties around ours. Finley refused because the property has been in our family forever, and it's home, you know?"

I nod.

She continues. "Finley held out long enough that Oliver sent in the big guns, a guy known for making deals happen. His name is Archer. Archer managed to make everyone happy with a joint-ownership deal between them. We got to keep our family home, and Finley agreed to convert the rentals into a camp for disadvantaged kids. And now Finley and Archer are together. He helps manage the property too."

"He likes the work?"

She purses her lips in thought. "I think so. Jake is hard to read, all he wants to do is make jokes and eat."

"It must be a fulfilling job—working with kids."

I considered going into social services when I was in college, because of the experience I had after my parents died. I was placed in emergency foster care for a couple days before they sent me to live with Aunt Moira and Uncle Paul. I was lucky. So many have no one.

"I love that they named it Camp Aria," I add. I didn't know her well, but Aria had the same glow Taylor did, the ability to light up any room with a smile. It was a shock when she died, the accident ricocheting through the community and leaving devastation in its wake.

Her eyes soften. "Me too. It was Finley's idea."

"How are the rest of your sisters doing?"

She bites her lip and I zero in on the movement.

Her eyes track over my face. "I don't want to talk about my family anymore." Her voice goes husky, the sound brushing against my skin.

My heart thumps in my chest, my body firing to attention.

She shifts in my direction, one of her hands lifting to trace a line from the tips of my fingers up the side of my arm to my shoulder, bringing herself even closer. The gold flecks in her dark eyes are mesmerizing. Intoxicating. The sound of her breath moving in and out between her parted, glossy lips is hypnotic. It would be so easy to get drunk on her.

My focus zeroes in on her mouth, the need to kiss her so overwhelming I have to physically fight to keep myself still. But I won't make the first move. She came here seeking shelter, and I won't take advantage—until I know for sure she wants me as much as I want her.

She lifts up on her knees, moving slowly but inexorably closer, swinging one leg over to straddle my thighs.

Breath whooshes out of my lungs.

My arms lift automatically, gripping her hips, my heart a hammer in my ears.

I can't believe this is happening.

I focus on her face, the heat in her eyes, the smile dancing around her lips.

Her hands squeeze my shoulders. "Is this okay?"

Unable to speak, I barely manage a nod.

"Good." She leans forward and presses her lips to mine.

CHAPTER
Three

TAYLOR

His mouth is soft. He tastes like afternotes of the bourbon we drank: oak and berries. Sweet with a hint of tartness. The kiss moves from warm to blazing in seconds, burning hotter than the fire heating the room.

When his tongue brushes mine, a groan rumbles up from the back of his throat, the sound triggering a response in my body as if he flipped a switch that has a direct line between my legs.

I grip his shoulders and lean in closer, pressing myself into his chest.

His fingers slide into my hair, gripping with silent possession.

He presses soft kisses down my jawline to my neck, the scruff on his jaw scratching against my overly sensitized skin sending erotic tingles through me.

He pulls back to search my eyes. "Is this okay? We've been drinking."

"I had one glass. I am completely in charge of my faculties. You?"

His head dips once. "Same."

"Then this is more than okay, it's fantastic."

"Good."

We shift and he lifts me up slightly, rearranging our bodies so he's spread out underneath me on the sofa, our legs entwined, and then we're kissing again, mouths moving in tandem.

I've never been so easily manhandled. Not something I would have thought of as a turn-on, but for some reason his strength combined with his attention to my comfort, the way he asked for permission to proceed . . .

It's all so *incredibly* arousing.

I pull back slightly. His lips are red and swollen from our kisses.

Addicting.

I dip my head and then we're kissing again.

I want to gorge myself on his lips, his mouth, the glide of our tongues.

This is the best foreplay I've had in years.

There's something so appealing about how he's this rough-and-tumble mountain man, but under the rugged exterior, he's sweet. Kind. Understanding. A good listener. And interested in what I have to say, his focus absolute and sincere.

Dammit, that's hot.

One of his hands stays in my hair, and the other smooths down my back, stopping just above my jeans against my lower back.

I wriggle against him, his length growing and hardening even through all the layers of clothes between our bodies.

I slide my fingers down the front of his shirt, skimming over his flat stomach, keeping one palm pressed on his chest. Shifting to one side, I brush over the insistent bulge in his pants.

His heart stutters under my fingers, his voice going ragged. "Taylor."

My name passes through his lips on a groan sparking a rush of pure female satisfaction. It's gratifying, having a giant who could crush me with one arm sprawled under me, relinquishing all control and enjoying the hell out of it.

"Atticus." My lips feather over his. "I want you."

Our eyes meet and lock, breath mingling. "I want to touch you first."

Who am I to turn down a man interested in my pleasure? "You don't have to threaten me with a good time." I shift further to lay on my side, lifting up my hips to help him.

Without hesitation, he tugs at the ties around my sweats and slips his hand underneath, encountering the first layer of clothes.

He pauses for a brief second before his fingers slide under the pants, encountering the thermals.

The corner of his mouth twitches. He pushes at the

thermals, encountering the final layer I tugged on before braving the storm.

He dips his chin in an attempt to peer between our bodies. "How many layers are you wearing?"

I toss back my head and laugh. "I'm sorry."

"Don't be sorry." His voice is laced with humor. "I like it, you're like a xerophyte." He's almost made it through all my clothes, his fingers rubbing over the silky fabric of my underwear.

My body goes nuclear at the delicate pressure, heat blazing through me, setting my nerve endings on fire. "A what?"

"In xerophytes, epidermis is present in a multilay-ered form. For example, a cactus." He pushes the many layers down to expose me to his searching fingers, his movements gentle but insistent.

I shift more to help him while trying to find the pieces of my mind that scattered around the room at his touch. "Are you comparing me to a prickly plant?"

He makes a *hmmming* sound in confirmation while his lips press gentle kisses and sucks along my neck. "In desert plants, it prevents loss of water in dry condi-tions." His voice is low and rumbly, his breath tickling my skin.

I shiver.

Finally, his fingers brush against the bare flesh between my legs.

He groans. "You're so wet." His voice is reverent as he carefully learns the contours of my body with the tips of his fingers, his eyes on my face monitoring every reaction, repeating certain movements when my response is more animated.

No one has ever paid so much attention to every hitch in my breath, every movement, every whimper and moan.

The arousal intensifies and I rock my hips, seeking more.

He immediately shifts his hand so the base of his palm rubs against my sweetest spot, while one of his thick fingers slides into me.

"Yes." The word is barely intelligible.

He leans in closer to kiss my neck, making a trail down to my shoulder.

I groan and my head falls back, allowing him greater access.

The press of his mouth combined with the slight abrasion of his calloused fingers, his palm rubbing between my legs, send me into sensation overload.

The tension in my body twists tighter and tighter and I can't hold it back.

A brilliant flare of pleasure crashes over me, nearly unbearable as it cascades again and again, my whole body contracting and then releasing me into a state of drowsiness.

Time becomes hazy, and when I eventually return to the world of the living, I'm tucked into Atticus's side.

His fingers rub a strand of my hair, a gentle tug on my scalp.

My limbs are languid from release. I'm half asleep.

It's been a long day and a longer week. I could dive into oblivion.

His deep voice rumbles against me. "One more. I want to taste." He shifts, sliding downward.

Aaaand I'm awake.

Holy shit.

Atticus came to win today.

He tugs down my clothes the rest of the way, tossing all of it to the floor, and then his broad shoulders wedge between my legs and . . . *oh.*

Oh my.

Piece by piece, he pulls me apart once more, one touch at a time, with every flick of his tongue and brush of his lips.

The world fades away and all that exists is his mouth and the receding pleasure ratcheting up again, filling every cell in my body, bit by bit.

He increases the tempo, adding his finger to the mix, moving faster and deeper, his tongue twisting around and around and then another finger joins the first.

A garbled scream escapes through my lips. My body arches, drawn as taut as a bowstring, and then I burst, stars exploding behind my eyes as the second massive orgasm blasts through me.

My body is wrung out. Completely spent. I blink drowsily down at Atticus, his head still between my legs while he sweeps gentle kisses against my inner thigh.

It's sweet. Sweet and dirty, my favorite combination.

The image grows blurry as my eyes droop shut, pulled down by heavy weights.

I should have slept more this past week.

Slumber overtakes me and pulls me into a dark, dreamless embrace.

I return to consciousness slowly, awareness returning to my limbs one at a time.

I'm covered by a thin, soft blanket, which is completely unnecessary because heat envelops the length of my back, radiating through the rest of me.

Warm air puffs against my neck. A heavy weight presses around my waist.

Weak light pushes through the curtains, coating the room in gray. A click sounds in the walls and the low hum of a heater fills the room. The power is back on.

I slip out from under Atticus's arm and then pick up all the various articles of my clothing scattered on the floor. Arms loaded, I snag my bag from the chair and then creep down the hallway in search of a bathroom.

Shutting myself inside, I plug my phone in the outlet on the wall, resting it on the dark granite counter. I take care of necessities—peeing, washing my face, rubbing toothpaste on my teeth—while my phone takes in some much-needed juice.

I need to call Finley and get out of here before Atticus wakes up.

He gave me multiple orgasms, and I fell asleep. My hands lift, covering my heated face.

I'm so embarrassed. And yet, part of me would have no problem waking him up for round two. Or is it three?

No. I can't do that. With the morning, sanity returns. I'm leaving in a couple of days anyway. A repeat performance would be awkward. Wouldn't it?

Besides, I hate saying goodbye. It's better this way. I'll probably never see him again.

Or by the time I see him again, years will have passed, and he'll be married and settled down with three kids, a blond wife, and a Yorkie with a perfect pink bow in its hair.

The thought generates a pang, deep down, but I shake it off, mentally scolding myself. Dramatic much? Clearly, I've gone way too long between hookups.

I need to get out of here. As soon as possible.

Keeping the phone connected to the charger, I dial Finley's cell.

"Hey, stranger. Merry Christmas Eve." The words are a little raspy.

"Did I wake you?" My voice echoes, bouncing around the small bathroom, even though I try to keep it low.

"Why are you whispering?" she asks.

I wince at my reflection in the mirror. Because I'm trying not to wake up the man who gave me multiple orgasms before I passed out on him. "I'm . . . I'm here, in town."

She gasps. "What? How did you get to town? When? Where are you?"

Before I can answer there's a murmuring from her end of the phone, a deep masculine voice talking nearby. Archer.

"It's Taylor. She's in town."

"I ran out of gas out on Maple Parkway last night in the middle of the storm."

"Last night? You got here last night? Why didn't you call?"

"My phone was dead, and the power was out. Besides, there's no way anyone could have come to rescue me in that monster storm."

A rustling accompanies her words. "You're probably right, although you know Jake would have tried. Where did you sleep? Please don't tell me you had to stay in your van all night in this cold."

"No, the bus died right outside of the Petersons', so I stayed at their place."

No need to mention the Petersons are out of town and only Atticus was here and everything else that followed.

"That is a relief. Tell Paul and Moira I said hi."

"I will." The next time I see them, which may not happen for months. Years. Whatever.

"Let me see if Jake's awake." She raps on his door and then it creaks open. "Hey, can you take the plow to go pick up Taylor?"

"Hell yeah," Jake says, loud enough that the words are clear.

I cover my mouth to stifle the chuckle.

Finley sighs. "Sit tight. Jake is getting dressed. He'll be there with a can of gas in no time. Archer is making French toast with croissants for breakfast."

I smile. "Sounds delicious. Tell Jake I'll keep an eye out for him. See you all soon."

"Wait, Taylor. Before you hang up, you should know that Mindy and Luke are here. They made it home yesterday morning before the storm hit."

My stomach squeezes, anxiety gripping me in a tight fist.

Mindy would have a field day if she knew about this little snowed-in escapade. At least, prior to last month, before she had some kind of come-to-Jesus epiphany, decided to apologize for treating me like crap for the past eight years, and now is so accommodating and careful, I don't even know what to do with it.

"It's fine, Finley," I tell her, even though it's not and we both know it.

We hang up and after releasing a deep breath, I finish getting dressed.

When I return to the living room, Atticus is still sleeping on the sofa, one arm stretched over his head. His features are softer in repose, less rugged, but no less appealing. My eyes follow a path from his tousled hair down the V-shaped line of his body.

A delicate thread of arousal wraps around my midsection and tugs.

I shut my eyes and turn away. *Stop being creepy, Taylor.*

There's a pad of paper and pen on the side table by the front door. I scribble a quick note before sneaking out.

Twenty minutes later, the snowplow rumbles to a stop next to my bus and Jake jumps out of the cab, grinning ear to ear. "Dude. This thing is awesome." He smacks the side of the plow.

I groan. "Boys and their toys."

"Right? Oliver had it delivered last month. Having a billionaire brother-in-law is totally worth having to deal with the egomania." He takes a few big steps in my direction and wraps me in a hug.

The zipper on his oversize jacket digs into my cheek but I don't even care.

He went through a rough patch a couple months ago, fell off the wagon, but today he looks good. Great, even, his eyes bright and clear, cheekbones tinted pink from the cold.

He reaches into the cab of the plow and pulls out a gas can. "Shall I do the honors, my lady?"

I roll my eyes and follow him over to the gas tank.

"Finley wants to make Christmas cookies today, so brace yourself." He lifts the can, pushing the spigot into the opening.

I groan. "Are you helping?"

"Nope. Not enough room in the kitchen." He tosses me a wink. "I'm going snowmobiling around the property with Luke, Oliver, and Archer."

"Seriously?" Which means I'll be hanging with

Finley, Piper . . . and Mindy. No thanks. "Can I go with you guys?"

"We only have two snowmobiles. We'll be riding butts to nuts as it is."

Irritation buzzes under my skin. I don't want to be in close proximity with Mindy. She'll be extra nice, and I'll be super annoyed.

Once he's finished putting the gas in my tank, I jump in the bus and start it up, then follow him into Whitby at five miles an hour.

The town center has been transformed into a winter wonderland, in part because of the snow, but also because of the small-town charm on display every year during the holidays. The antique black lampposts lining the street are adorned with giant red bows and winding garlands. Shop windows are decked out in window art, reindeer, snowmen, and Hannukah menorahs.

It's quaint. It's beautiful. It's home.

It should be perfect. So then why do I want nothing more than to keep on driving, the urge an itch scratching under my skin?

At the gas station, I pull up to the pump and wave to Jake as he continues down the road back in the direction of home, plowing the road as he goes.

I fill up my tank and then jump back into the driver's seat, but before I can put the bus into first gear, my phone dings.

I found you a potential lead out of
northern California. Call me.

It's from Georgia, a private investigator I hired last month.

She has a lead.

My heart jumps in my chest.

She's been sifting through state and county vital records throughout the country, searching for women who legally changed their names from Rebecca Fox.

I stare at the text.

Two paths roll out in front of me.

If I leave now, I can make it to sunny California in a week.

Or I can spend Christmas with my family, including having to put up with more of Mindy's apologies, forced good cheer, and sad eyes, not to mention Finley trying to maneuver us into getting along.

My stomach turns at the thought, the buzzing agitation increasing until it's a swarm of wasps desperate to escape.

Ugh.

I scroll down my list of texts and click on Finley's name, thumbs hovering over the keyboard, staring at the blinking cursor for a minute before typing.

I can't. I'm sorry. I'm heading out west for a show. I'll call tonight. I love you.

I click send, shut off my phone, and toss it into the passenger seat.

Grabbing my bag, I slip out the picture from the side pocket. It's black and white and faded with age and the press of a thousand fingertips. The woman in the photo is laughing, her head thrown back, neck exposed, revealing a Phoenix pendant nestled against the lower part of her throat.

The only picture I have of our mom.

I tuck it back into the pocket.

I need music. Something happy and upbeat. After pushing some buttons on the iPod, Poor Man's Whiskey fills the bus, the strains of "Lake County Lady" chasing away my lingering irritation.

Putting the bus in first gear, I turn my mind away from Whitby and toward California. The drive will be slow, impeded by the snow even with the plows out in full force.

But with each passing mile the itch ebbs, decreasing in strength until eventually, it's just me and the music, and the rest is behind me.

CHAPTER

Four

Vibrations reverberate through the house, rattling the windows and rousing me from a dead sleep. I sit up and the distant hum recedes, leaving me staring blankly at the empty pile of ash in the fireplace.

I'm on the couch.

A wave of memories from last night crash over me.

Taylor.

The living room is empty, all the millions of layers of clothing she was wearing that I tossed on the floor last night are gone. My ears strain for sounds from the kitchen or down the hall, but it's silent.

She's gone.

I should be disappointed that last night ended in unsatisfied arousal on my part, at least, but instead, I find myself proud that my exertions were so successful they effectively wore her out.

She was amazing. It was incredible.

After she snuggled into my chest and promptly fell asleep, I ignored my raging hard-on and covered us with a blanket from the back of the couch.

Maybe I should have gotten up and gone to my own bed, or let her sleep alone, but her hands were fisted in my shirt, even in sleep, with her face burrowed into my chest and her legs wrapped around me like a vine.

Her slight weight was comforting. I breathed in her scent like she was a Félicité Parmentier rose, exotic and sweet.

With a sigh, I rock to a sitting position, swinging my legs to the floor. My eyes snag on a piece of paper left on the side table by the front door.

I stalk over to it.

Thank you. Sorry.
 XOXO
 Taylor

I laugh, but the sound turns into a groan. Of course I have one of the most incredible nights of my life with a woman who immediately bails.

My phone rings.

It's a video call from Aunt Moira.

I scrub my hands through my hair and answer, plastering a wide grin on my face. "Hey."

"There he is!" Moira's and Uncle Paul's beaming faces fill the narrow screen. Behind them, Sylvie and Marika are squeezed into the back of the frame, Sylvie waving excitedly while Marika grins.

"How is Bermuda?"

Moira squints at me, her eyes focusing somewhere over my head. "Wait. Are you home? I didn't think you would make it."

"I got in yesterday, right before the storm rolled in. I didn't think I was going to make it either."

Moira's eyes widen. "You're going to be alone on Christmas."

Paul frowns. "Maybe there's a last-minute flight out today or tomorrow? You could still make it and spend the holiday here with us."

I shake my head. "It's fine. I have to leave the morning after Christmas anyway. I'll hang out here and get some rest before I have to hit the road. I hope you all are having a great time though."

Moira frowns, but then forces it into a smile. "Your present is under the tree. Open it any time you like."

"Thank you."

She waves a hand. "Of course."

Moira and Paul always buy me random "helpful" things they see on TV. I've received everything from a tactical pen to a food dehydrator. One year I got the Clapper. They even installed it in my room.

We chat about their plans for the rest of their vacation and how they'll be getting back to Whitby late the night after Christmas.

After we hang up, I shower and head to the kitchen to scrounge up some breakfast.

It's quiet. Too quiet. I glance at the empty seat by the island, where Taylor sat last night and wolfed down her sandwiches.

The silence is deafening. It's like her mere presence brought vitality into the space and now she's gone and the life left with her.

I open the fridge, peering at the nearly bare shelves.

Other than condiments, there is half a block of cheese in a drawer, a carton of expired milk, and a package of bacon.

I glance at the clock. It's eight in the morning. Woody's, the only grocery store in town, will be open until eleven. They always are on Christmas Eve. It'll be a slow drive through the snow, but I have nothing else to do.

Fifteen minutes later, I'm cruising the crowded deli section for some ready-made meals for myself over the next couple of days and for my family so they don't come home to a nearly empty kitchen.

The Christmas spirit in Whitby is tangible, with frequent eruptions of "happy holidays" and boisterous laughter echoing through the aisles.

I'm surrounded by people, most of whom I know vaguely. They nod and smile and wish me a happy Christmas. And yet, a sense of isolation wraps around me like a cold hug. I'm in a crowd and yet still somehow not a part of it.

Story of my life.

I reach for a ham and cheese deli sub, breakfast of champions, at the same time as someone else.

"Sorry."

Dark eyes meet mine, eyes that look almost exactly like Taylor Fox's, because they belong to her eldest sister, Finley Fox.

"Hey." Before I can stop myself, the words fly out. "Did Taylor make it home safe?"

She throws a puzzled glance over her shoulder at the person behind her, a tall, dark-haired, flannel-wearing man who is maybe an inch or two taller than me.

A wrinkle forms between her brows. "You are . . . ?"

I stick out my hand. "Atticus Stone. She stayed at my family's house last night."

Her face clears as recognition hits and she reaches for my hand to give it a firm shake. "Oh! You're Moira's nephew, right? I don't think I've seen you since you and Taylor graduated from high school. This is my partner, Archer Weston." She motions to the man towering behind her.

I nod. "Nice to meet you."

He smiles and then shoots Finley a quick look before saying, "Taylor is fine."

Finley ducks her head. "Well, she made it *somewhere* safely. We hope. She didn't come home. I think she went traveling in search of warmer climates." Her voice is dry. "Anyway. Are you getting some last-minute items for family dinner?"

I rub the back of my neck. "Not really. My family went to Bermuda for Christmas."

She frowns. "Oh." The single syllable is laced with a combination of concern and confusion.

Ah. Maybe Taylor didn't mention it was only the two of us.

"It's fine. I had work, and I have to hit the road again early tomorrow morning." I shrug it off.

"Work?" Archer asks. "So soon after the holidays?"

"I have to evaluate some vegetation down in Florida."

Finley's head cocks to one side. "That sounds interesting. What kind of work do you do?"

"I'm a field botanist. I do botanical surveys and environmental inspections for utility and construction companies."

Her mouth pops open. "Really? That's amazing."

Archer leans closer, his hand resting on Finley's shoulder. "I imagine you'd have to be good at hiking and outdoor things and the like for your work?"

I nod slowly. "Um. Yes."

Finley's eyes trace over the contents of my shopping cart, which has beer, frozen lasagna, and ice cream, and her lips purse. "So, uh, what are you doing for Christmas dinner, since your family is gone?"

I shrug. "No plans."

She and Archer exchange a glance and then Finley speaks. "I have an empty seat if you're interested. You'll have to put up with a cranky billionaire, a lot of insanity, and Jake's bad jokes."

Archer chuckles, squeezing Finley's shoulder. "If anything, it will be entertaining."

"I'm not sure. I don't want to intrude."

Finley reaches out to touch my forearm. "Please. It's the least we can do since you helped Taylor out yesterday."

It would be better than being alone. It's not like I have anything else to do.

I nod. "Count me in."

CHAPTER
Five

Taylor

I knock on the half-open door before nudging it open the rest of the way. "Hey there, megafamous rock star."

Luke is alone, sitting on a wooden bench, with his guitar in his lap and legs stretched out in front of him, his cowboy boots propped up on a stool.

He grins, setting the instrument to the side before standing and crossing over to draw me into a hug. "Hey, you. I'm so glad you could make it."

"Wouldn't miss your debut for anything."

His brows lift, nearly hitting the shaggy, dirty-blond mop of hair brushing over his forehead. "Despite the fact that you'll likely run into my better half?"

I wince but force my mouth to curve into a smile. "I am a master of avoidance. I'm not worried about it."

We're in the back room of the Mercury Lounge, a small but vibrant indie venue on the Lower East Side.

It's the first night of Luke's upcoming tour. My sister Mindy signed him to her record label, and they are newly dating. Even though Mindy and I aren't on the best of terms, Luke is already like a brother. He's sweet, charming, charismatic, and has a killer voice.

He tilts his head and considers me, his eyes gentle. "Forgiveness doesn't mean ignoring what's been done or minimizing your feelings about how you were treated. It takes a strong person to say they're sorry, and an even stronger one to forgive."

I knew he would stick up for her, but the words sting anyway. "I guess I'm a weakling."

He winces. "I'm sorry. I shouldn't have gone there, it's not my place, I know that, and you are completely within your rights to smack me upside the head right now, it's just—"

I wave a hand. "I know. You love Mindy. You want her to be happy. I get it."

"I do, but I also want you to be happy. I owe you so much. We wouldn't be here if it weren't for you."

"That's not true."

"Well, we wouldn't be here as quickly if it weren't for your intervention."

I duck my head. "It was no big deal."

Luke and Mindy were working on his first album when the producer she had arranged bailed. I hooked them up using some of my connections from the festival circuit.

Mindy had had no other options at the time because so many in the industry refused to work with her due to some stupid scandal with one of her clients, a very married musician.

I change the subject. "Tell me about your upcoming tour. Where are you going next?"

We chat for a bit, and then I leave him to prepare for his upcoming set, heading back out to the front of the building, where the audience is waiting.

It's a small show. The only people invited were close friends and family of Luke and Mindy.

I'm rounding a corner in a narrow hallway near the stage when I run into someone coming in the opposite direction.

"Sorry. Oh." Mindy startles when her eyes lock with mine, lifting a hand halfway to her mouth.

Great. I guess I'm not the master of avoidance.

I grit my teeth and shift to move around her.

"Thank you for coming." Her voice is soft with sincerity.

Crossing my arms over my chest, I keep my gaze over her shoulder. I can't look her in the eyes, the same dark, expressive eyes that Jake has. That Aria had.

"I came for Luke." *Not for you.*

"Right." She ducks her head. "I know he appreciates it."

I step around her.

"Wait, Taylor."

I sigh but come to a stop. It would be immature to stomp away like some kind of preteen. I can take the high road.

The high-ish road.

"What?"

"I wanted to thank you for everything you did with Ursula and Laila, and if you ever want to . . . I don't know, work in the music industry in any capacity, I would be happy to introduce you to people or return the favor in any way I can."

I stare at her. What is she expecting from me? She treated me terribly for years, and now she wants to act like it's all fine, like the past can be erased, like the ache from her sharp words, drilled into me time and time again, no longer matters. Like those wounds have healed without leaving scars. "If that was something I wanted to do, I wouldn't need your help."

She winces. "I'm sorry. Forget I said anything."

I blow out a breath, irritation crawling over me like bees on a honeycomb. "You don't have to keep doing this."

"Doing what?"

I flick a hand at her. "Being all nice or whatever. It's weird."

"Taylor, I don't want it to be weird. I want to be nice to you."

"It's great you've made your peace with all the crap you put me through, but I haven't. Can't we ignore each other?"

She takes a breath and releases it before speaking. "I

get it. I was terrible. I can respect your wishes and leave you alone if that's what you want. I won't talk to you unless strictly necessary."

Even though it's hurting her. The remorse is etched into the frown marring her face.

A sliver of regret pierces me in the chest, but I shove it down and harden my resolve. Mindy never cared about all the times she hurt me. Why should I care now? This is nothing more than karma.

"Perfect." I step around the corner, ready to escape this entire conversation, but then the crowd comes into view and my eyes land on a familiar face.

A familiar, handsome face.

The face of the man who gave me multiple orgasms before I promptly fell asleep and then cut and run the next morning with nothing more than a three-word note.

"Shit." I pull back behind the corner, out of sight of the audience beyond the stage. My heart gallops in my chest.

I haven't been back home since Christmas and one of the big reasons is standing out in the crowd, next to Finley.

What is he doing here?

Embarrassed heat rolls through me. Our night together was one of the most intense experiences . . . ever.

And then I bailed.

So long and thanks for all the orgasms.

Mindy's brows furrow. "What are you doing?"

I peek around the wall. "Nothing." I pull back again.

Damn, he looks good. Even better than the rose-colored memories I've been trying to forget.

"It's nothing. I'm fine," I repeat. I don't know who I'm trying to convince more. Mindy or myself.

"It's obviously not nothing." Mindy steps past me, scanning the audience. "Who are you scared of?"

"I'm not scared of anyone."

"Then go out there." She gestures.

I can't control it. I glance out into the crowd again, picking out Atticus's head easily since it's above the rest of the room before I draw back again.

Mindy's eyes follow my gaze, then sharpen. "Are you avoiding Finley?"

Damn nosy siblings. "No."

"Is it one of her employees?"

Employees? Finley mentioned she hired some counselors and scientists for the specialized camps, and that she would be bringing them to New York to combine some kind of team building with Luke's show.

But does that mean . . . is Atticus *working* for Finley? For my family?

My stomach dips like I'm in an elevator and it hit the bottom floor.

If Atticus is working at the camp, we will cross paths every time I go home.

What if he hates me? Does Finley know? Did he tell everyone how we . . . ?

No. No way. Of course he didn't tell them. Finley would have said something. Jake would have given me so much shit. I would never hear the end of it. Do I have to talk to him? I have to at least clear the air. I can't let my family sense anything amiss.

"Hey. Who's the big guy?" Mindy points, her words cutting into the panicked thoughts swirling around me like a tornado.

I follow the line of her finger.

Of course she would immediately zero in on Atticus.

His head turns and he looks straight at us.

I grab her arm and yank her back behind the wall and out of view. "Could you be any more obvious?"

She bites her lip, ineffectively hiding her amusement. "Is he an ex-boyfriend?"

"No," I snap.

"Do you wish he was?"

I groan and cover my face with both hands.

"It must be something juicy if you're willing to spend extra minutes with me to avoid him."

Laughter bubbles up in my throat, and I cut it off with a cough. I don't want to be amused by Mindy. I don't want to remember how close we were, once upon a time. "Ugh. You are the literal worst."

Straightening, I stalk past her, down the side of the stage, and through the gathering crowd, losing sight of him amongst the revelers.

Might as well bite the bullet. The longer I wait, the weirder it will be when we inevitably encounter each other again.

An assortment of colognes mixed with a whiff of stale beer assaults my nostrils as I wind through the clumps of onlookers, moving in the general direction of where Atticus was standing.

What am I going to say? Hi, how are you, thanks for all the orgasms, sorry for running away?

"Taylor!" Finley tugs me into a hug. "There you are. Jake said you were here. I thought maybe you already left."

She doesn't say *again*, but the word echoes in the air between us anyway.

Finley's mouth is spread in a smile, but there's strain around the edges.

"We've been having such a great trip. Oliver met all the new hires and he behaved almost like a normal human."

She launches into some story about the first spring camp scheduled for April, and I half pay attention and half keep a side-eye out for Atticus.

Where did he go?

I hate that things are weird with Finley. I want to tell her everything. About Atticus, about what happened, about the mom search, but I can't. I've created this wedge between us.

What is it about guilt and family and how you can't have one without the other? Or is it just us?

"I have to pee." The words erupt from my mouth, overly loud, cutting Finley off while she rants about Oliver and his inability to compromise over something with the camp.

Her mouth freezes, half open.

I spin around and run into a broad chest, assailed by

the faint scent of cedar mixed with fresh soap.

Atticus. His hands cover my shoulders, warm and familiar.

I force myself to meet his gaze. Our eyes lock and fire zings down my body, sparking over my skin.

Arousal splashes over me like he just turned on a horny shower.

"Hey, there . . . you." I clear my suddenly dry throat. "It's, uh, so nice to see you again." I finish with a super cool light arm punch.

Someone stop me before I make it worse.

CHAPTER
Six

ATTICUS

"It's nice to see you too." I duck my head and lower my voice. "Empress of Awesome, was it?"

It's the lamest joke I've ever made to anyone, ever, but her eyes light up and she releases a surprised chuckle, the outcome worth the risk of humiliation.

She's wearing a flowy, long-sleeved bohemian dress with a chunky silver necklace and high, fringed boots. My mind explodes with images. What would she look like with only the boots and those long legs wrapped around my hips?

I swallow, hard.

Her eyes widen, cheeks highlighted pink. "I'm surprised to see you here."

Finley didn't tell her that I accepted a job with Camp Aria.

Before I can respond, Eve steps up beside me, her arm brushing mine.

"Is this Taylor?" She sticks her hand out smiling broadly. "I've heard so much about you from your family. It's so nice to finally meet you."

Finley motions to Eve. "Eve is one of our new instructors. She just got accepted into a PhD program in astrobiology, so we have her until next term when she goes back to school. And of course you know Atticus, he's one of our full-time staff now. His botany background is perfect for the science and hiking retreats."

Taylor nods, her eyes darting to the minuscule space between me and Eve before she asks Eve more about her field of study.

Eve laughs at something Taylor said, leaning closer into my side, and nudging me with an elbow.

I smile down at Eve and then meet Taylor's narrowed eyes.

Is that jealousy in her gaze? No, it can't be.

Eve and I only met a couple of weeks ago, but she's been flirtatious, dropping some hints that she might be interested in a less platonic relationship.

Eve is intelligent and kind. She's also attractive in a classical way, with her straight blond hair, bright blue eyes, and pearly white smile, but there's no spark. Besides, we work together. I'm technically her boss, and she's moving across the country in six months for her doctorate.

People across the room clap, the sound spreading like a wave to the rest of the room.

Luke takes his place on the stage, waving at the crowd and sitting up on a stool with his guitar in his hands.

He adjusts the microphone and then leans forward to speak. "Thank you everyone for being here tonight, the very first night of my very first tour."

The crowd cheers, shouts echoing to the ceiling.

"I appreciate every person in this room tonight, all my friends and family here to help send me off. I would be remiss, though, if I didn't take a moment to thank the person who's responsible for us all being here tonight." His gaze points over at the corner of the stage. "I wouldn't be here today if it wasn't for one woman. Mindy, I don't know what I did to deserve someone who taught me not only to believe in myself but to believe in love. This one is for you."

The crowd gives a chorus of *aww*s.

Luke strums his guitar and then he sings, something about waking up and missing something real.

It's slow and sweet, and clearly written for Mindy.

Eve shifts on her feet next to me, only a few inches on my left. Taylor is on my other side, a couple of feet away, arms crossed over her chest.

Even though Taylor is farther away, the air between us simmers with electric tension.

The first song ends to a chorus of raucous cheers and whoops. Luke switches to a faster, livelier tune and the crowd goes wild.

Finley jumps up and down, jostling Taylor and shoving her into my side.

Our arms brush and electricity sparks from the point of contact through the rest of my body, the reaction immediate.

"Sorry," she murmurs.

I nod and face forward, hyperaware of her every breath and twitch.

Energy crackles where our arms are separated by a mere inch.

My heart pounds so hard, the beat must be echoing through the room in time with the beat of the music.

Our fingers brush.

It's only a second. Maybe less than a second, but something in my chest clenches and releases.

It was an accident. Must have been.

But then she shifts closer, and our hands brush again, and this time, she doesn't pull away.

Neither do I.

The entire room goes fuzzy. Forgotten. Inconsequential. It's only me and Taylor and the centimeter of her skin against mine.

It's nothing and everything.

I'm thrown back in time to the sofa, Taylor half naked and spread out in front of me like a decadent buffet. My scalp prickles at the memory of her fingers clenching in my hair.

My body tightens and hardens.

I want her more than I want my next breath.

The song ends, and Luke croons another slow-paced love song. A few couples sway onto the dance floor.

Archer sweeps by us, grabbing Finley by the waist. She laughs in delight as he spins her away.

The draw of having her in my arms again is too strong to resist. I hold out my hand to Taylor. "Dance?"

After a second's hesitation, she takes it.

Her fingers lift to my shoulders, sliding in near my neck. "So. How exactly did you come to be working for my family?"

My hands lower to her hips, gripping gently. "I ran into Finley and Archer at Woody's the morning after— ah, the morning after your bus ran out of gas. They invited me to Christmas dinner."

Her brows lift. "You ate Christmas dinner with my family?"

I duck my head to speak closer to her ear. "Finley asked me to dinner, then she asked me to head their science camp division. I supervise some of the other counselors. You didn't know?"

"No." She shakes her head. "I've been . . . I haven't been home in a while. Things have been busy."

Her eyes pause for a second over my shoulder. One of her eyebrows lifts, the corner of her mouth twitching.

"What is it?"

"Your, uh, friend, Eve. If looks could kill there would be a filet-o-Taylor all over this lovely concrete floor."

"A filet-o-Taylor would be a terrible thing."

Her eyes flick to the side and then back to my face. "Is there something there I should be concerned about? Am I going to get jumped when I leave the room?"

I shake my head. "No. It's not like that."

"Something tells me it *could* be like that."

I search her eyes. Her tone is light and teasing, and yet . . . she *is* jealous.

The knowledge is selfishly gratifying. "It might be like that for her, but I'm not interested."

Her fingers clench on my shoulders. "Why not?"

I press my lips together to suppress a smile. "We work together. And I'm her boss."

"And if you didn't work together?"

I shrug. "I don't have any feelings for her. Not in that way."

She bites her lip. "But she's hot. You don't have to have feelings for someone for it to be something."

Is she mentioning a meaningless hookup because that's what we were?

"That's not really my style."

"Hmm." Her eyes flick in Eve's direction again. "You might need to let her know that."

"Are you jealous?" The question tumbles out before I can stop it.

She meets my gaze head-on, her brows furrowing. "I have no right to be."

You could have the right. I swallow the words before they can expose me.

It would never work. I live in Whitby, she lives wherever the wind takes her. Jake and Finley have made enough comments about Taylor's adventurous spirit and nomadic tendencies, the way she's always on the move, always seeking the next party.

The song ends and she gives me a sad smile, slipping out of my arms. "Maybe I'll see you."

And before I can utter another word, she disappears into the crowd.

CHAPTER
Seven

Taylor

Finley answers after the first ring. "Taylor? Is everything okay?"

I sit down on the curb, stretching my legs out in front of me into the empty street. The light above me flickers and then clicks on. It's nearly eight, the sun descending over the horizon, but there's still enough light to read the sign on the corner, *Pearl's Garage Service & Repairs*.

"I'm good. I'm really glad you got me that roadside assistance package with towing for my birthday. Did I thank you for that? Thank you for that."

There's a burst of chatter in the background, a

chorus of high-pitched voices laughing and talking simultaneously. "What happened? Where are you?" Finley raises her voice over the noise.

"The bus broke down. I'm outside of Pearl's shop."

Pearl is the town mechanic. She can't be a day under seventy, always dyes her hair bright pink, speaks at a decibel just below an ambulance siren, and has worn the same blue coveralls with the nametag of "Frank" since sometime in the last century.

"Oh, good. You're nearby. We'll come get you. Jake, can you make a run to Pearl's? Taylor is there."

Jake rumbles something, too far away for me to make out the words.

"Hang on a sec," Finley says. "Let me get out of the mess hall. We're keeping the kids occupied until the sun sets for the night activities. It's like herding kittens who have been injected with caffeine and laughing gas." A few seconds later, a door shuts and the noise cuts off and Finley exhales. "Sorry for the noise. It's been a long day and we're slammed over the next week. We have two groups, one with teens and another, larger group of middle schoolers."

I pick at a stray thread on my overnight bag. "I'm sorry to cause any inconvenience."

"Nonsense. You could never be inconvenient. I didn't mean that as a complaint. We have more than enough staff to handle everything here. Honestly, I know you would rather be on the road, but I selfishly hope it takes Pearl more than a little time to fix your van because I miss you."

Guilt squeezes me by the throat. "I miss you too. You might get your wish. I have a feeling I'm going to need a lot of funds to pay for these repairs. I'll go see Veronica tomorrow." Veronica owns a bar and grill outside of town. She was friends with Dad before he passed. We've known her our whole lives. She always lets me pick up shifts when I'm in town and need some extra cash.

"Sounds good. Jake is on his way. He'll be there soon."

"Thanks, Finley."

"See you soon. Love you."

We hang up and I slip my phone in my bag and gaze down Main Street, taking a deep breath of the mountain air, filling my lungs with the fresh scent of pine and dirt —plus the underlying notes of oil and rubber from the garage behind me. Still, a definite improvement from where I spent the past week, at a festival inhaling the odors of stale beer and urine, combined with a heady mixture of the great unwashed.

The last time I was here, Main Street was drenched in Christmas spirit. Now flower baskets overflowing with spring colors adorn each lamppost lining the street, sprinkling Whitby with little pops of purples, reds, and yellows.

Two blocks away, a couple spills out onto the sidewalk outside the Eager Beaver Diner, laughing and holding hands.

I tuck my legs into my chest, wrapping my arms

around my knees. I'm home. Again. Living with family because I'm basically homeless.

I turned twenty-seven last month. I'm on the downward slide into thirty, and what do I have to show for it? A broken-down bus, zero accomplishments, and nothing more than a shoebox full of old tickets to concerts and festivals, gathering dust in a cupboard.

Five years ago—hell, one year ago, my life was perfect. I was never bored. Traveling, living my life on the go, always meeting new people. Exploring new places was the epitome of living life to the fullest.

Now . . . I don't know what it is. The endless parties have gone stale. I've been chasing after the high I used to get from being in a crowd, surrounded by people, and now the same activities leave me empty.

It isn't helping that all attempts to locate Mom have led to dead ends. Maybe I should give up. Get a real job. Join a cult. Like a normal person.

A Jeep with the camp logo on the side slows to a stop against the curb about ten feet away.

I stand up and grab my bag.

The door opens and a broad figure jumps down.

Shit on a shingle.

Atticus.

We're ten yards away from each other, and the intensity between us reaches out and snags me by the waist.

What happened to Jake?

He comes to a halt a foot in front of me. His scent drifts to me on the slight breeze, soap and aftershave.

"Hi," I say. The best conversational gambit at my disposal.

"Hey. Can I help you with your bag? Did you have anything else you need?" He glances behind me to where the tow truck driver left the bus parked outside the bay doors.

"No. It's fine. This is all I've got. I'm used to traveling light. Thanks, though."

He ducks his head in acknowledgment, shoving his hands into his pockets.

I take a second to size him up. He looks good. Really good. The night air is warm enough for a T-shirt and jeans, exposing his broad shoulders and muscle-laden forearms.

Why did I run away from him again?

Stop staring. Eyes up. I jerk my gaze to his face.

His lips press together, suppressing a smile.

Heat floods me from head to toe, half embarrassment, half the crackling fire in my belly that leaps toward Atticus whenever he's within touching distance. I clear my throat. "Where's Jake?"

The smile he's been holding back breaks free. "He sent me as his errand boy."

The grin takes his features from handsome and tosses them into downright striking.

My mouth goes dry. I clear my throat to speak. "Why am I not surprised? Although I doubt those are the words he used."

"You would be correct. He prefers to call me his favorite little beyotch." He chuckles and turns away, holding the passenger door open for me.

I chuck my bag in the back and then we settle in our seats, awkwardness sitting between us like a third passenger. Twitchy, I reach over to fiddle with the radio, putting on the local oldies station.

"While My Guitar Gently Weeps" takes over the unease filling the car, eating through the silence, and I settle back in the seat.

Am I anxious because I'm sitting inches away from a man more tempting than sin, or because I'm finally heading home for the first time in six months?

My stomach churns with guilt.

Maybe it's a combination of both.

I didn't mean to stay away quite so long, but since last Thanksgiving, the thought of being home makes my chest constrict, like I'm stuck in a vise sinking to the bottom of the ocean. So much is changing for my family, while my life has gone stale. The cabins where I used to play hide-and-seek with Aria are being torn down. My siblings are all busy with their lives. And then Mindy—I cut that thought off at the knees.

I don't want to think about her. I would rather make cringe-worthy small talk. "So. How are things?"

He clears his throat. "Things are good. You?"

"Well, they could be better, considering my bus is crapped out in front of Pearl's."

The corner of his mouth tips up, and he nods once.

I turn my gaze out the window. Towering trees soar into the sky on either side of the road, capturing the encroaching gloom and pressing shadows onto the road stretching out in front of us.

We pass Veronica's, aglow with lights, the parking lot half full. Busier than normal.

A mile later, he turns off the main road onto the narrow drive leading into the camp.

I keep my gaze focused out the passenger window for a glimpse before we turn up toward the main house.

I catch a quick glimpse of white fairy lights, weaving around tree trunks and hugging the edges of rooflines, before the scene disappears from view.

Wow. Just that little glimpse was incredible. I've missed so much.

Atticus rolls to a stop in front of the porch of the main house. It hasn't changed much on the outside, other than the porch being redone last year. The two-story structure is a hodgepodge of materials, from red brick to dark wood with a smattering of stucco thrown in for good measure. It's weathered and misshapen and I love it for all its oddness.

"Are you getting out here?" I ask.

"No. I'm dropping you off. I have a class coming up." He peers out the windshield into the night sky.

"At night?"

"When it gets a little darker. Stargazing and s'mores making." He faces me, dark eyes locking with mine.

My stomach tumbles at the connection.

How am I going to resist him for the next however long I have to be in Whitby? It's going to be at least a month. Maybe he would be open to a little fling. Just to get it out of our systems. Then I'll leave and everything will go back to normal.

"Atticus, I—"

My passenger door swings open, making my heart jerk, and then Jake's familiar form scoops me out of the seat and swings me around.

"Tay-tay!"

I shriek in surprise, the shock quickly turning into laughter. "Jakey!" He puts me down and I smack him on the arm. "You scared the crap out of me."

He rolls his eyes. "That was kind of the point. I see Ace brought you home without any problems."

"Ace?" I glance over my shoulder at Atticus.

He's watching us from the car, a small smile playing around his lips.

"He needed a nickname, and Fuckwad has already been taken." Jake shrugs.

I lift my brows at him. "And why did he *need* a nickname?"

"Who wants to call someone Atticus all the time?" He cringes.

I stick a hand on my hip, slightly outraged in his defense. "What's wrong with Atticus?"

"It's too long. At-ti-cus. That's three syllables. Three. It's exhausting and ridiculous. Now, Ace. Ace is simple. Easy. Quick. So when I need to call him, I don't have to expend a lot of effort and energy."

"Do you hear this guy?" I jerk a thumb at Jake.

Atticus sighs. "Every day."

Jake puts his hands on his hips. "I'll have you both know that I am a delight."

I chuckle. "We're all aware." I grab my bag from the back seat of the Jeep and give Atticus a smile. "Thanks for the ride. Good luck with the kids. Is Finley down at the camp?"

"Yes. She and Archer both. I better get back. See you both down there."

The taillights disappear around the curve in the driveway, and I loop the crook of my arm in Jake's. "So. Tell me everything I've missed."

"Archer is a dick." We stomp up the porch steps together.

"No, he isn't."

Archer is the last person on the planet I would describe as a dick. He's kind and considerate and cares more about Finley than anything else in the world, including himself. I couldn't have asked for a better match for my sister.

"I haven't had a drink in eight months and he still acts like I'm a toddler about to tumble into a vat of whiskey with every step."

I chuckle. "He loves you."

"That's even worse." He groans in faux pain and opens the front door, motioning for me to enter the house before him.

"Wow. The office is . . . it's so different." I glance around. A year and a half ago, the space was cluttered with old furniture, a desk from the dark ages that was scuffed and damaged, and an ancient PC with a barely functioning keyboard. Now, there are two desks both with brand-new, state-of-the-art flat screens, the furniture has all been updated, the old shag carpet has been replaced with warm woods, and the walls have been painted a chorus of beige and pale blues.

"After Archer and Finley finished this space, they went to town in there." He jerks his head in the direction of the interior door that leads to the rest of the house.

"They didn't get rid of the wood paneling, did they?"

It's old and outdated, most people would remove it, but without it our house wouldn't be like home.

"Nope. Come look."

We go through the door from the office that leads into the open-concept dining and living room. The new flooring extends in here.

I toss my bag on the dining table and amble into the living room, eyes trailing over the varying shades of gray bricks set around the fireplace, the white-washed wall where they've painted over the wood siding, and the new teal-colored furniture. "Wow. It looks good. We've never had furniture that actually matches. I can't believe how much has changed in a few months." Okay, so maybe it's been over six months, but still. I sit on the couch, bouncing a little. "Did they just reupholster this? It's still really lumpy."

Jake throws himself down next to me. "I found out something about the letters."

"What?" Letters? What is he talking about? My

mind takes a moment to catch up. "Oh, those letters. The ones we found—"

"Yeah. Dad's letters."

I slump back, rubbing my head.

After Thanksgiving last year—the last time I was home—we went through Dad's room together as a family to clean it out. It was past time. Dad's been gone for seven years, and yet his bedroom had remained untouched.

We haven't even discussed Aria's room yet, and it's been over a decade since she passed. That's a wound that might never heal.

The letters were written by someone named Ryan, and the topic in most of the letters revolved around a "Mia." No one has any idea who Ryan or Mia are. Frankly, I don't want to know. The thought of Dad having some kind of clandestine second life leaves a sour taste in my mouth and an uncomfortable twist in my belly.

Even though I have secrets of my own.

The picture of Mom I keep in my bag? I found it when we were cleaning Dad's room. It was in the bottom drawer of his dresser. I hid it from them, but I couldn't stop looking at her photo and wondering about her. That's when I hired Georgia.

Jake angles in my direction. "So anyway, I think I found something that might help us find who the letters are from."

"What did you find?" I tuck my legs under me, wiggling to get comfortable.

Jake rubs the bristles on his chin. "I think I know where the letters are coming from, at least geographically."

When we found the letters and Jake wanted to be the one to research their origin, I didn't think he would take the task seriously. He doesn't take much seriously. "How did you figure that out?"

"There was a sentence that didn't make sense, 'Good old Dull.' I thought it was a mistake or something, but then I realized there's a town called Dull in Oregon."

My brows lift. "Dull, Oregon? Seriously?"

"Yep."

"So you think the letter writer lives there?"

He shrugs. "Or they used to. It's a small town, and these letters were written almost ten years ago. I've tried searching around online for any Ryans or Mias living in Dull, but I don't have last names. I don't know, do you think it would be weird to reach out to people who live in the town to see if anyone knew Dad or these people in the letters? I don't really know where to begin, or what to say even if I found someone who knew something. What do I even ask?"

I purse my lips in thought. "You could hire a private investigator."

"To do what?"

He doesn't know I've gone down this route myself, and I'm not about to tell him. "They can find things not available on Google or social media. Skip tracing, image searches, databases the public can't readily access, property records, marriage records, address records, all of it."

His head tilts. "How do you know all that?"

"I banged a PI once at Lollapalooza."

He groans and covers his face. "Taylor."

"What?" Okay, so it's not entirely true, but I did meet Georgia at Lollapalooza. She agreed to give me a discount for her services after I let her sleep in my van during stormy weather when her tent sprang a leak.

"I did not need to hear that."

I giggle and smack him on the knee. "So. Have you told Finley?"

His hands drop to his lap. "No. She's been busy with the camp. You're the only one I've told."

Probably because the rest of our siblings are all wrapped up in their work and their relationships. Over the past year, they've been coupling up at record speed. It's like Love Island without the island and much grosser because they're my sisters.

He taps my knee. "How long are you staying?"

"Until I can get the bus fixed."

He frowns.

"Don't give me that hangdog face. It will be at least a few weeks, probably longer. I'm going to see Veronica tomorrow about work. I need to save up some money, so you won't be getting rid of me anytime soon."

"Good." His eyes soften. "I've missed you, Tay."

I slide toward him on the couch so our shoulders press together. "I've missed you too."

We sit there for a few seconds, then he elbows me

away. "No more sappy shit. Come on. Finley is dying to see you. Let's go down to the camp. You can help with the kids' science stuff. You'll love it." He jumps off the couch.

I follow him through the kitchen and out the side door. "How am I going to help with teaching kids anything?"

He glances at me over his shoulder. "C'mon, you've gleaned many skills over the years. You can show them how to dress like a wookiee, make flower crowns, and pee in the woods."

I laugh and shove him in the back. "Dick."

"You love it."

I really do.

We head down in one of the camp golf carts. The night air is bracing against my cheeks as Jake rounds a curve between the cabins, taking us to the center of the property where the firepits and mess hall are located.

I get a better view of the camp up close, more than just the white fairy lights. Stout wood cabins are arranged in scattered intervals underneath the looming pines, along with the cobblestone street rumbling underneath us, all of it transforming the night into a glowing, hobbit-like wonderland.

A swell of emotion clogs my throat and I swallow it down. I'm so proud of Finley and Jake, of everything they've accomplished, and how hard they worked to turn our family property into this magical fairyland. But underneath the pride is regret.

I shouldn't have stayed away so much. This last stint was the longest, six months. I've missed out.

Jake parks outside the firepit. Finley and Archer are in the middle of a swarm of kids, while a smattering of counselors valiantly attempt to herd the children into the mess hall.

The adults stand out, their heads above the kids, all wearing the same matching blue zip-up hoodies, the logo for Camp Aria emblazoned across the front.

Involuntarily, my eyes search the group, but there's no sign of Atticus.

"Taylor!" Finley extricates herself from the center of the small group, making her way through the gaggle of elementary-aged kids.

She flings her arms around me, encompassing me in the scents of home, like dirt and pine and a hint of soap.

She steps back and Archer is the next to wrap me in a giant bear hug. "Hey, Taylor. We're glad you're here."

"I'm happy to be home. Everything looks so different." I gesture behind me. "Finley, the house looks amazing. All of it does."

She beams. "Thank you. They're all finishing up s'mores and then heading into the mess hall to make lava lamps. Want to sit with me out here for a bit and catch up?" Her eyes are hopeful.

"Absolutely."

A few noisy minutes later, the campers have been herded away by counselors, Archer bringing up the rear of the group and squeezing Finley's hand before he leaves.

Jake claps a hand on my shoulder. "I'm going to check out the stargazing. They're up on the hill if you want to stop by later." He tilts his head toward the hill that juts up between the camp and the pond on the other side of the property.

"Stargazing?" I sit on one of the benches, stretching my fingers out toward the fire.

Finley takes the spot next to me. "Atticus and Eve are doing star maps with some of the older kids. Tonight was the perfect night since it's a new moon and the skies are clear."

"Ah." Eve. The woman at Luke's show. She stuck to Atticus like glitter sticks to everything and looked like a kicked puppy when Atticus and I danced together.

He said there was nothing there, but it's been months. I wonder if they're dating now. Maybe they've hooked up. My stomach squirms at the thought.

Ridiculous. I'm the one who left. I always leave. I can't be counted on to be anyone's . . . anything.

If I'm being real, deep down inside, he scares me a little. I'm not a safe kind of person. I'm wild, free, unfettered. Safe sounds great to most people. Security. Shelter. A soft place to land. For me, standing still is terrifying.

Tossing thoughts of Atticus to the side, I focus on catching up with my sister. I tell Finley about the past few months, and she gives me the lowdown on everything I've missed including updates on my siblings and their significant others.

"Oliver really hung up on you?"

"To be fair, I called him a fuckwad with the emotional maturity of a jellyfish."

I throw back my head and laugh. "And what did Piper have to say to that?"

"That because of her hard work, his emotional maturity is at least hamster level."

"She does love the fool."

She sighs. "And he loves her too, in addition to making her deliriously happy so I can't totally bag on him, as fun as it is."

Oliver and Piper are polar opposites. He's a cranky, brooding billionaire and she's an artistic genius who creates brilliant metalwork sculptures and a sweetheart to boot.

"I'm trying to get them to come to Whitby to visit while you're here. They are always so busy."

"That would be great. I would love to see both of them."

"It's been, what, four months?"

"Yeah about that. Since Luke's show in the city."

Archer sticks his head out of the door to the mess hall, the sounds of children laughing and talking leaking out into the night. "Babe, where's the Alka-Seltzer tablets?"

"They're in the cupboard above the art supplies."

He leans a little farther out the door. "Are you sure? I looked there."

"Did you do a man-look?"

He groans. "I'll check again." The door shuts, wiping out the noise of the kids.

"Man-look?" I ask.

"Seriously. The man can spot a hawk flying in the sky three miles into the distance but ask him to grab the ketchup out of the door of the fridge and he's suddenly blind."

I chuckle.

She shifts toward me. "Uh, speaking of Luke, Mindy might be in the area next week and—"

"No." I lift my hand.

She reaches out and taps my fingers. "You didn't even let me finish."

I cross my arms over my chest. "I know what you're going to say, and if Mindy is coming home to visit, let me know when and I can make myself scarce."

"But Taylor—"

I stand. "I'm going to go find Jake."

"Really?"

"I'm sorry, Finley. It's been a long day, and I can't right now. Go help Archer find the Alka-Seltzer. I'm not mad at you, I just . . . I'm not ready."

Spinning away, I head in the direction Jake disappeared.

I don't want to think about Mindy.

Turning my face to the sky, I take a deep breath and exhale to let out all the negative energy that Mindy's name incites. The stars are out, stretched overhead in a tapestry of twinkling lights.

Voices and laughter echo on the breeze. Following the sound, I take the path leading away from the camp, meandering up the incline.

Where the hill crests, a couple of groups are clustered around two telescopes set about twenty feet apart.

Atticus sticks out like a skyscraper in the center of a field of stumps since he's two heads taller and twice as broad as anyone else up there, including Jake.

He's bent over one of the scopes while a couple of smaller forms crowd around him. He steps back to let one of the kids look into the eyepiece.

"Taylor." Jake waves at me, drawing my attention.

Jake is standing by the other telescope with a group of three teens, more sitting on a felled log behind him.

I head in his direction, sneaking one more glance over at Atticus.

He's a few feet away from the crowd of kids at the telescope, talking to one of the other teachers.

Eve.

Atticus says something and she laughs, throwing her head back in mirth and reaching out to put a hand on his arm.

My stomach lurches and I force my attention back to Jake, my stride more purposeful.

He's not mine to yearn for, and yet I'm burning for him anyway.

CHAPTER
Eight

ATTICUS

My stomach dips, awareness wringing my every nerve ending.

Taylor glances at me from twenty feet away, no more than a shadow in the darkness, and my entire body bursts into flames.

Eve follows the direction of my gaze and then chuckles and pats me on the arm. "I'm going to check on Ryder and Nathan."

I nod, forcing my gaze away from where Taylor is peering into a telescope.

Next to her, Jake gestures broadly, talking to some teen campers sitting on a log who are documenting their findings on slim tablets, the glow illuminating their faces.

I make my way over to their telescope, unable to resist the pull of her voice on the breeze.

Up close, her features come into sharper focus. My eyes track over some of the details that have stuck with me since I picked her up at Pearl's. There are violet smudges under her eyes, and her cheeks are more pronounced than they were four months ago. Has she lost weight? Is she not sleeping well? Concern nibbles at me.

"What is money called in space?" Jake asks the group.

Taylor groans and covers her face with a hand. "I cringe to ask."

One of the kids pipes up. "What's money called in space?"

Jake grins. "Star bucks."

Two of the girls sitting on the log crack up.

Jake points at them. "See? It's funny."

Taylor shakes her head.

"You think you can do better?"

Taylor props one hand on her hip, eyeballing Jake. "Why didn't the dog star laugh at the joke?"

"Why?" I ask.

Taylor smiles at me. "It was too Sirius."

I chuckle, and she catches a couple of laughs from the kids.

Jake frowns. "I don't get it."

"Sirius," she repeats. "You know, S-I-R-I-U-S, also known as the dog star."

"Dog star?" He scoffs. "Like that's a real thing."

"Aren't you supposed to be teaching them about the names of stars and constellations and whatnot? Wouldn't it help to actually know something?"

"Don't get all mean because your joke wasn't funny."

She scratches her nose. Was that her middle finger? "At least it was actually science related."

"Maybe that's what made it suck."

She smacks him on the arm.

I clear my throat before speaking. "What do you say if you want to start a fight in space?"

Jake claps his hands once. "Here comes Ace with a zinger. Sorry, but you can't win here. Taylor and I have been telling each other bad jokes since we were in diapers."

I lift my brow at him. "Comet me, bro."

Taylor laughs, the sound free and unfettered, and even in the dim light, the planes of her face shadowed, it hits me like an arrow in the gut.

"Hilarious, Ace. Really, you should have been a comedian instead of a plant nerd."

Taylor releases an exaggerated sigh and spins toward the girls. "Will you show me what you're working on?" She perches on the log next to Trinity.

"Let's look for the cat star." Jake leans over the telescope.

"There is no such thing as a cat star," Taylor calls out.

He twists around to look at her. "You said there's a dog star."

"There is."

"Where?"

She groans, stalking over to the telescope and nudging him out of the way.

He steps to the side. "If there's a dog star, there should be a cat star. Am I right?" he asks the kids, but then his head whips back in Taylor's direction. "Dude, what was that? Was that your stomach or did the ground just vibrate underneath us?"

She leans away from the telescope. "Yeah, it was me. I haven't eaten since this morning."

"Why didn't you say something when we were at the house?"

She shrugs. "I forgot."

His face contorts in mock horror. "How could you forget to *eat*?"

She sighs. "It's been a long day."

I take a few steps closer to them. "I can drive you back to the house."

"Perfect." Jake jerks a thump toward the campers. "Eve and I can get them back to camp before lights-out."

Taylor hesitates, but then her stomach groans again, so loudly the nearby campers laugh. "Fine," she says.

When we're heading down the hill toward the cart, she nudges me with her elbow. "So I guess my stomach being obnoxious and you feeding me when my bus breaks down is like our thing."

I chuckle. "I guess it is." We reach the cart and I lift

up the back seat to grab one of the camp sweaters stored there and then hand it to her.

"Thanks." She takes it, our fingers brushing, sparks flaring up my arm from the contact.

The chilled night air brushing between us doesn't do anything to mute the heat.

"Thanks for driving me . . . again. You could have made Jake do it."

I shrug. "He likes to stay up late with the older kids. Keeps him distracted."

Her gaze hits the side of my face, the weight of it almost a physical caress. "Did he tell you that?"

"He did." I glance over at her and our eyes lock for a penetrating second.

I quickly aim my gaze at the road ahead.

I've grown closer to Taylor's family over the past few months, especially Jake. Life dealt him some shit at a young age, and under the bravado, he's just doing his best to get by. The camp, the kids, and all the activities are the perfect distraction from his relentless demons. Nights are the worst for Jake. It's when his thoughts are the loudest.

"You've gotten close with my family."

I peek over at her again, gauging her reaction since her words had no inflection. Her words mirror my thoughts so closely. "Does that bother you?"

"No," she answers quickly. "Not at all. Did you tell them about," her hand waves in the air, a motion I catch out of the corner of my eye, "us?"

Ah. "No. I suppose this means you haven't told

them anything either?"

She chuckles. "No."

"Right."

It was one night of passion. We're both adults. It's no big deal, right?

I bring the cart to a stop in front of the main house, an echo of when I dropped her off earlier.

"Thanks." She shifts, turning to face me, her face shadowed by the glow of the porch light behind her. "So." She bites her lip. "Do you want to come inside? We could, ah, eat together, or something?"

"Or something?"

She gives me a slow smile in response.

An intense jolt of lust hardens my length immediately, pressing against the fly of my pants like the organ has a direct connection to her words.

Clearly, the answer my body wants to give is *hell yes*.

But something holds me back, and I'm not sure I can articulate it. She's leaving. I'm staying. Will this make things weird since I work for her family? The same family that will be arriving back at the house within the hour. Maybe she's not suggesting what I think she's suggesting.

"Are we really talking about food?"

She leans toward me. "Food. Sex. Yes. A fling might be fun, while I'm here. Don't you think?"

I swallow. "What about Jake? He'll be home soon."

She blinks. "Maybe later tonight, then? What cabin are you staying in? I can come to you."

My hands tighten around the steering wheel,

wishing for the first time I was living on site. "I'm staying at home. I've been housesitting."

"Your family is gone?"

"Paul and Moira are home now, but they're leaving again in a couple of days."

Her head tilts. "Again?"

"They're spending their retirement traveling across the country in their RV but they come home now and then."

Her lips purse in thought. "That complicates things." She sticks out her hand, palm up. "Let me see your phone."

Unable to refuse her anything, I shift to tug my cell from my pocket, unlocking it and then handing it to her.

She keys in her number. "Call me when they're gone. We can finish what we started last December."

"I thought you were starving." Jake's voice jolts through me. "Why are you yahoos still sitting outside?"

"Uh." Taylor twists in the seat to face Jake, walking up the drive. "We're just talking about how," she glances down at my phone, still in her hand, "I'm going to give Atticus a reading. I got new tarot cards when I was in Sedona earlier this year."

Jake groans. "She told me the last time she trapped me into one of her woo-woo readings that I should avoid sombreros, goldfish, and west-facing windows. Seriously, don't let her get you into it."

"Oh, you are definitely getting into it," she murmurs, low enough for only me to hear.

My gaze flies to her face, her eyes gleaming, her smile wicked.

"So call me. For the *reading*. Whenever you're free." She winks, handing me my phone before hopping out of the cart and ambling over to Jake.

"Come on, brat, make me a chicken salad sandwich." Taylor loops an arm over Jake's shoulder.

"See ya, Ace," Jake calls out, tossing me a wave.

He turns back to Taylor and murmurs something that makes her laugh.

A distant pang echoes through me at their shared laughter, the closeness they have, the connection nearly palpable. I don't have any siblings.

Since my parents died, I've been an outsider everywhere. Part of the group, always invited, and yet somehow still an interloper, even with my own family.

I leave the keys in the ignition of the golf cart and make my way to my truck parked on the side of the house.

Ten minutes later, I'm home. The house is dark. Moira and Paul are in bed. Still sitting in my truck in the driveway, I scroll through my contacts, searching under *T*.

Huh. Her name isn't there.

I browse the list starting at the top, and a laugh barks out of me when I find it.

She put herself in my phone as "Empress of Awesome."

I chuckle. Getting involved with Taylor might be the best decision I could make—or the worst.

CHAPTER
Nine

Taylor

"You've got some big problems, honey." Pearl throws the words at me over her shoulder as I follow her away from the garage.

"Tell me something I don't know." The scents of metal and oil and burnt coffee make my nose twinge as we head down a short hallway that leads to Pearl's office.

The high-pitched whine of tools and mechanics shouting at each other fades when she shuts the door.

She rounds the desk, pulling out a file from the drawer and slapping it on the cluttered desk next to a stained mug that reads *real cars don't shift themselves*. "The engine is toast. It needs to be replaced. You been getting the oil changed like I told you?"

"Sure."

Nope.

Pearl sighs, inured to my lies. "I can order the parts now. It will be a little bit of time to get them shipped in and do the work."

"How much do you think this will cost me?" I hold my breath.

"A lot."

My stomach twists, despair swamping me. I plop down in the dark green guest chair, the peeling vinyl in the seat cushion scratching my upper thighs. Can this day get any worse?

I'm stuck in Whitby for the foreseeable future. It's only a matter of time before I'm itching to go, and I won't be able to leave.

The old leather chair behind the desk emits a creaky groan as she sits. "The parts cost about three thousand dollars. With labor, you're looking at about five thousand all in."

Shit.

A small fortune. But not insurmountable. I don't have any debt. The bus is paid for. My only financial obligations over the past several years have been general maintenance on my traveling home—which I have clearly slacked on—car insurance, gas, food, and festival entrance fees. Some of those things I do temporary work for, others I obtain by bartering and sharing expenses with friends I've met along the way.

"That's with the friends and family discount," Pearl continues. "I'll let you know when the parts arrive, then you let me know when you have the money, and we can get started." She keeps talking, going on and on about manifolds and carburetors and gaskets and whatnot and the words all run together into gibberish.

"What's your plan?" Pearl's question snaps my attention back to her.

I blow out a breath. "I'm going to go see Veronica about a job."

She points at me. "Smart. Tell Veronica she owes me twenty dollars from last week's poker night."

At two o'clock on a Tuesday, Veronica's should only have a handful of vehicles in the lot, but when I park the Jeep next to Veronica's MINI Cooper, half the spaces are taken.

The bright sun beats down on my shoulders as I make my way to the building.

I wait by the doors as my eyes adjust to the dim interior. My eyes trace over the high ceiling, past the plethora of dark wood coating every visible surface, down the L-shaped scuffed wooden bar top, and to the pictures cluttering the walls: everything from old photos of downtown Whitby from the 1950s to a pale green retro sign that reads, "Life is uncertain . . . eat dessert first!"

I've worked in a variety of bars and restaurants around the country over the years to fund my lifestyle, usually under the table. Some have been decent, others have been downright hellish, but no place is like Veronica's. It's more than a building, it's comforting and familiar. Like a home away from home.

We hung out in the bar all the time when we were kids. We'd eat all the cherries and orange slices, help her sweep the floors, and dust the bar.

On the wall next to the door, there's something new. I peer at the framed record. Luke's first gold album.

"There's my girl!" Veronica's voice rings to the rafters as she hustles out from behind the bar.

She envelops me in a hug, her long silvery hair brushing against my face when she presses her lips to my cheek. "Pearl called." She pulls back, her hands on my shoulders. "You didn't change your oil, did you?"

I grimace.

She chuckles. "Well, from what Pearl said you'll be paying the price. Now let me look at you." The line between her brows deepens and her lips purse. "Oh baby, you're too skinny." She tsks.

I glance down. I suppose I have lost a little bit of weight. Over the past few months, every time I thought about how I ditched my family at Christmas, about Mindy's apology, about my search for our mom and basically *anything* related to my family, my stomach would tie itself into knots. So, daily.

I tried to outrun the anxiety by keeping myself busy, traveling from one festival to the next, one party to another, but now I'm just exhausted. And starving.

"Are you hungry? The lunch special is a turkey melt with mango chutney, Monterey Jack cheese, and avocado. We also recently added Irish nachos to the lunch menu."

My mouth pops open. "Are you serious? You've done more than a few updates around here. No wonder it's busier than normal."

"Oh, there have been a lot of changes since last year. Come on, let me put in an order for you and then we can catch up."

I follow her over to the bar and sit at the end, the same stool I always take when I come to chat with Veronica. I am supposed to be having family dinner in a few hours, but I can't say no to Veronica's food, especially since she's kicked up the menu a notch.

She writes an order on a notepad and sticks it on the order wheel, smacking the counter to get Daphne's attention, then walks over to where I'm perched on the stool.

"You want a drink, honey?"

"Water is fine. Tell me what's up with the new gourmet menu items."

She grabs a pint glass, the silvery bangles on her wrist jingling as she scoops ice into it and then fills it with water using the soda gun behind the bar. "It's been a little bit busier since Luke's show. Some of those music people liked the area enough that they've come back a few times, and they've told their friends. They already go to the Catskills for skiing, so they're nearby anyway. They didn't even know Whitby was here." She chuckles, setting the glass of water in front of me.

I take a sip. Mindy made sure to include some big-name influencers in the audience the night Luke played here. She did more than drum up buzz for Luke's album release, she got Veronica some return customers.

"That's great."

She nods and then claps her hands together. "And it's a good thing you are in town and looking for work, because Rachel is due next month with my first grand-baby, and I wanted to stay with them for a week to help with the baby shower."

Veronica's son, Adrian, lives in Connecticut, about a three-hour drive away.

I nod in agreement. "Of course. I would be happy to do whatever you need."

"You are a lifesaver. I'm not leaving until Friday, so maybe you can come in during the day and focus on the paperwork until then?" She presses her hands together like she's praying.

I grin. "You need me to clean you up again?"

Veronica hates the business side of her, well, busi-ness, and every time I work for her, I help her sort out paperwork and balance her books so her accountant doesn't freak out at tax time. I don't mind doing it. It gives me a sense of accomplishment, taking something disordered and putting it to rights. Plus, I love making Veronica smile.

She chuckles. "You know me too well. But I wanted to ask you for a little more than that."

"Order up," Daphne calls, setting a plate towering with food on the pass-through window.

Veronica takes a few steps over to grab the plate and then sets it down in front of me.

"This looks great." I pop a sweet potato fry in my mouth and chew before asking, "What's the 'little more'?"

"I'll pay you more to manage the bar while I'm out." She lifts her brows in question.

I freeze with the sandwich halfway to my mouth. More money is essential to getting back on the road, but . . . "Manage?"

"Daphne takes care of the kitchen without much interference. We hired a couple more staff, one in the kitchen and one to help with the bar and the table service, so you'd only be in charge of four people."

I take my bite and chew, thinking it over. "And none of these other employees is interested in being in charge while you're out?"

"Gloria has no interest in management. She's retired and works here part-time in the evenings. Vanessa," she jerks her thumb over her shoulder to the waitress taking an order on the other side of the room, "has a kid. She can't work nights except for weekends. You're already going to do the paperwork, which is half the management job anyway."

"What's the rest of the job?"

She shrugs. "Posting the work schedules, putting out fires if someone calls out, ordering supplies, most of which you've helped me with before."

I have done all of that, but always when Veronica was here to fall back on. But it is only a week. "I don't know. Are you sure it's a good idea?" What if I mess things up?

"I'll show you the ropes before I leave. You'll be fine. You know this bar almost better than I do."

I can't say no to Veronica, and she knows it. "Fine. I'll do it."

Her eyes twinkle, her eyes wrinkling around the corners. "That's my girl. Come back tomorrow around ten and we'll get started."

At least this is something to distract me until I can leave again.

CHAPTER
Ten

TAYLOR

"Don't get angry," Jake says before I set foot inside.

I frown. "Why would I get angry?"

He grabs my arm and pulls me further outside, but not before familiar laughter rings through the kitchen, coming from the direction of the living room.

My stomach lurches at the sound. "Is that Mindy?" Finley told me the night I arrived she would be in town "next week," but it's only been three days. She didn't warn me.

He shuts the door, blocking the noise. "You said you wouldn't get angry."

I cross my arms over my chest, my entire body going rigid with exasperation. "I never said anything. *You* said not to get angry."

He waves a hand. "Semantics."

I groan, not sure whether to laugh or cry. "You are so annoying."

He grins. "Good. Direct all your anger at me, and then maybe we'll survive this dinner. Wanna punch me? Right here." He points at his chin, ducking slightly to get into my eyeline.

I tap his face with my palm. "Yes, I do, but it doesn't matter because there is no way in hell I am having dinner with her."

He frowns. "We got Archie's Pizza though."

"So?"

"It's your favorite."

"I'll take some to go. You can't make me stay." I want to stomp my foot like a toddler, but I restrain myself. Barely.

The side door swings open and Finley steps out. "Taylor, I was going to tell you."

I prop a hand on my hip. "Tell me what? That you were setting me up?"

She shakes her head. "That's not what happened."

"You said she wouldn't be here until next week."

"I'm outta here." Jake slips back inside.

Finley takes a few steps closer, her shoulders so tense they nearly hit her ears.

I get where she's coming from, and it's not Finley's fault Mindy and I are fighting. She loves both of us, and she's been stuck in the middle of this feud for years, a feud that never would have happened if Mindy hadn't lashed out at me the way she did. But Finley should have warned me. I could have stayed at Veronica's for dinner.

Finley reaches out, pulling me into a side hug. "She's truly sorry. She's trying."

I don't return the motion, my arms stiff at my sides. "Too little too late."

She steps back to meet my eyes. "So you're what, *never* going to forgive her?"

My jaw clenches so hard I might break a tooth.

She doesn't understand.

It's easier to hold on to the anger than probe at the wound, and poke at the feelings the anger is masking.

Aria is dead, and it's still my fault.

"I'll forgive her if I want to, and when I'm ready, not when she or anyone else demands it. Not even you."

She winces, her tone immediately apologetic. "Taylor—"

Gravel crunches behind me.

Atticus's truck rolls to a stop next to the house, and Atticus's large frame unfolds out of the driver's seat.

"Hey." He turns to grab a box from the passenger seat and ambles over. "Sorry I'm late. I grabbed the pie you asked for." He glances between us, taking in my rigid stance and Finley's strained features.

He's wearing khaki shorts and a blue camp tee that outlines his broad shoulders and is just a little too tight on his biceps.

Why does he have to be so damn hot?

I squash down the attraction. It's been three days since I last saw him, and he hasn't called.

"Hey, Atticus." Finley frowns at the box in his hands. "Um. I didn't ask for a pie?"

"Jake said—" He cuts off and his eyes fly heavenward with a sigh. "Jake duped me into buying the pie. He said it was for you because he knew I wouldn't get him another one."

My brows lift. "Another one?"

Finley laughs and the tension weaving around us dissipates slightly.

Atticus sighs. "I've brought him six."

"How has he managed to con you six separate times?" Finley presses her lips together, holding back a smile.

"Because I'm a sucker."

Finley chuckles, patting Atticus on the shoulder. "That sounds about right. We can all enjoy the pie together after pizza. You're staying, right?"

He nods. "Absolutely."

She turns to me. "And you?"

As much as I would prefer to run away, I suppose can manage to sit through one dinner and ignore Mindy.

I blow out a breath. "Yes. Of course I'm staying." I'll just ignore the anger trying to shove its way up my throat and the insecurity from Atticus's rejection twisting knots in my belly.

I'm used to repressing emotions.

Inside, I follow Finley toward the voices chattering away in the dining room.

There are four large pizza boxes resting at the top

of the massive oak dining table, along with a stack of paper plates, napkins, cups, and a pitcher of lemonade.

Mindy, Archer, and Jake are standing around near the food.

"You brought my pie." Jake takes the box from Atticus.

"*Your* pie?" Finley's eyes narrow on Jake. "I think this is *my* pie. He said you asked him to get it for me." She plucks the box from his hands, pulling it back out of his reach.

Jake stares down at his empty hands, mouth open. "Why would you do this to me?"

Archer slaps him on the back. "You'll survive. Have some pizza."

Finley sets the pie next to the rest of the food.

Jake picks up a plate and flips open a pizza box. "I love pizza, but it can never fill the pie hole."

"Technically, pizza is a pie." Archer reaches around him, grabbing a slice.

Jake frowns. "Says who?"

Archer pulls out a chair and sits. "Um, everyone. Haven't you heard the term pizza pie? It's circular, there's dough, what else could it be?"

Finley groans. "Is this going to be like the hot dog thing?"

Jake throws himself into the chair next to Archer. "A hot dog is not a sandwich."

Archer shakes his head. "It's meat between two slices of bread. How is it not a sandwich?"

"Uh, because it's a hot dog?" Jake takes a giant bite of his pizza.

I manage to snag a chair at the table between Jake and Atticus, as far as I can get from Mindy.

Organized chaos ensues as everyone gets their food and drinks and settles in around the table.

Once we're all seated, Finley turns to Mindy. "How is Luke?"

She dabs her mouth with a napkin. "I'm meeting up with him in Denver in a few days for his next show. He's been selling out the venues, so we added tour dates in twelve cities. We're going to start production for the next album this fall. He's been writing like crazy."

Against my better judgment, I glance over at her. Her smile is luminescent, her whole face aglow as she talks about Luke.

They are truly happy. It's written all over her face and in the sound of her voice. I could reach out and touch it.

Resentment boils in my gut. Why does she get to be happy after causing me so much misery for so long?

Then there's the jealousy. I wish I could find someone who complements me, like the rest of my siblings, all of them coupled up and excessively content.

Jake belches.

Well. Except Jake.

"How are things going around here?" Mindy asks.

"Good. This round of campers leaves in three days and then we have a wilderness survival camp in two weeks to prep for. Which reminds me." Finley nods toward Atticus. "We need to scope out the area for the hike up to Mayberry Falls. See how much the melting snowpack has affected the trail. This group is fourteen to sixteen, so they might be able to manage a little more difficulty."

Atticus nods. "I can check it out next weekend so it's closer to their arrival date."

"Perfect. Take Jake with you."

Atticus dips his head in assent.

"Hiking?" Jake grimaces. "Doesn't anyone else want to go?" He glances around the table, brows lifted.

"I'll bring snacks," Atticus tells him.

Jake purses his lips. "I guess I'll allow it. None of that healthy crap though, or I'm out."

Finley rolls her eyes and then looks at me. "How was Veronica's today?"

"It was good. I got most of her paperwork in order from the past six months. I swear she hasn't touched it since the last time I was here."

Mindy clears her throat. "Finley mentioned you'll be running the bar this weekend. You're so good with people. I bet you'll be a great boss."

My scalp prickles with uncomfortable agitation.

"Thanks." I give a tight smile but don't meet her gaze.

Kiss ass. Does she think throwing out compliments is the way to get me to forgive her? "Jake, can you pass the parmesan?"

We eat, the conversation ebbing and flowing with

other topics, and the tension in my body creeps toward relaxed normalcy.

Until Mindy clears her throat and tries again. "So how was Summerfest? See anyone good?"

How did she know I was at Summerfest? Are Finley and she talking about me?

Of course they are. They're my siblings, for better or worse.

I can't believe she's going to ask me inane questions and pretend like nothing is wrong. Irritation tightens my chest. Frustration burns under my skin, making me fidget.

"No." The word snaps out of me before I can restrain the strength of my response. "I'm not doing this with you, Mindy."

Silence stretches around the room, enfolding everyone at the dining table in the most awkward hug in the world.

Only Jake is immune. He reaches across the table and snags another slice of pizza from one of the boxes, taking a giant bite.

I'm incapable of pretending like things are fine when they aren't. They haven't been fine, not in a long while.

Finley watches me, her eyes sad.

I shove down the guilt like I always do.

I'm done pretending everything is okay when it's not.

I don't want to be in the same room with Mindy, let

alone make polite conversation while our family hangs on every word—probably so they can talk about it later.

Mindy pushes back her chair and stands. "Sorry, uh, excuse me, I told Luke I would call him when I got in, and I realized I haven't checked in yet." She offers a tense smile to the table, avoiding eye contact with me, and then disappears up the stairs toward the bedrooms.

Once her footsteps recede, Finley turns to me with pleading eyes. "Taylor, if you'd just give her a chance—"

"It's not your choice to make," I snap. I swallow and then stand. "I'm sorry. I . . . I need some air." I stalk into the kitchen and exit through the side door.

Outside, I take a deep breath and then head toward the dirt path that leads around the property line. The sun won't set for another hour at least. I need to burn off the emotions battling in my chest: anger, shame, and frustration mixed with a wallop of embarrassment.

Finley always takes Mindy's side. I shouldn't be surprised. They're only a year apart, Irish twins, Dad used to call them.

Mindy and I used to be close. The closest out of all my siblings, despite the five-year age gap.

I walk faster, rounding a slight incline, enjoying the burn in my muscles—a balm to the fire raging under my skin.

I hate the way my relationship with Mindy has been. I want to forgive her, I just can't. I'm too mad. Mad that I showed her my shame, gave her a piece of my guilt, and she stomped on my heart for years and now she gets to decide it's all good? It's not fair.

Maybe I could have handled dinner better. With a bit more maturity. God, what must Atticus think?

If he wasn't going to call before, he definitely won't now. Is there anything more unattractive than acting like a petulant brat during family dinner?

Embarrassed heat floods through me. I basically threw myself at his feet and offered my body on a silver platter and he ghosted me.

I'm a moron.

I wish I could leave. Just jump in my bus and go. But I can't, not for another month or longer. So instead I pick up the pace and run along the dirt path, faster and faster. I run until my muscles burn and my lungs ache.

But I can't outrun myself.

CHAPTER
Eleven

ATTICUS

When I agreed to dinner and drinks at Veronica's with some of the other counselors, I did not expect it to be only me and Eve.

"Where is everyone?" The bar is packed. It's a Friday night, but it's still more crowded than normal. The tables are all taken, but we manage to get a booth in the corner large enough for the five in our group . . . and three of them aren't here yet. Eve told me they had agreed to meet at six. It's six fifteen and it's still just the two of us.

"They'll be here," Eve says. "I'm sure they're running late."

Across the bar, Taylor emerges from the kitchen, carrying a tray of plates.

I also didn't expect Taylor to be our server.

My chest goes tight at the sight of her, my breathing suddenly shallow.

Her hair is scraped back into a ponytail, a few strands coming loose around her face. She's wearing a navy blue tee that hugs her curves, along with dark jeans and a waitress apron wrapped around her hips. Hips I've held in my hands. Hips I could hold in my hands again, except I still haven't called her. And it's been five days since she gave me her number.

"Before the others show up, there's something I wanted to talk to you about."

My gaze snaps to Eve.

She rubs her shiny lips together and smiles at me, the motion tremulous.

Is she nervous?

Her hair is down, flowing in waves around her face. She's wearing a scoop-neck black top that shows a hint of cleavage.

My stomach drops to my toes. Did she dress up because she thought this was a date? No. We talked it out, months ago, and agreed to be friends.

Things have been normal between us . . . haven't they?

"What is it?" I ask.

"I know you aren't interested in a relationship, and I'm not either," she rushes to explain, reaching over to rest her fingers lightly on my arm for a second. "I'm going back to school in a couple of months anyway, but I wanted to let you know—"

"Hi, Eve, hi Atticus. Thanks for waiting and sorry for the delay." Taylor approaches the table with a strained smile, plucking a pen from behind her ear and holding a black notepad in front of her. "We have a great spring menu we're offering tonight. There is a Mediterranean farro salad with seasonal veggies, fresh deli sandwiches, and a charcuterie appetizer with imported cheeses, artisan crackers, and fig jam that is to die for."

"No burgers?" Eve asks.

Taylor winces. "The oven is out of commission, temporarily."

"Oh, that's bad luck," Eve says, frowning.

Taylor sighs. "You're telling me. This whole night has been a series of unfortunate events."

"What happened?" I ask.

She blows out a breath and one of the loose strands of hair wafts up into the air in front of her face. "Daphne's daughter broke her arm. She had to take her to Binghamton, Eddie is sick, Gloria was scheduled to be off for her anniversary, and I have no idea what is wrong with the oven." She tucks the pen back behind her ear and rubs her temple.

"Do you need help with anything?"

Taylor smiles, the first real smile I've seen all night. "No. But thank you. Are you two ready to order?"

"Not yet. Waiting for the rest of our group." I motion to the empty seats.

Taylor nods. "Can I start you with some drinks while you're waiting?"

Is that relief in her gaze because Eve and I are not on a date alone, or is that just what I want to believe?

I can't imagine the offer still stands since I've let the silence drag on too long. I don't know how to tell her the truth of why I haven't called, without sounding like a complete moron.

"I'll take a water."

After a second of thinking, Eve says, "I'll have a dirty martini."

Taylor nods. "I'll come back when the rest of your people get here."

"Thanks, Taylor," I say.

She walks away with a wave, collecting dishes from an empty table and checking on other customers nearby. I can't tear my eyes away. I'm completely absorbed by the way she weaves through the tables, her arms loaded with glasses and plates and yet she's as graceful as a dancer.

"So anyway . . . Atticus?"

I tear my eyes away from Taylor to meet Eve's questioning gaze.

"About what I said before. I wanted to warn you."

"Warn me?"

"Yeah, uh—"

Stewart slides into the booth seat across from us. "Hey, sorry we're late."

Eve curses under her breath.

He's followed immediately by Patrick who sits next to me, his bright gaze darting between Eve and I. "Did we miss anything?"

"No," Eve answers quickly.

Patrick's brows lift.

"The menu is limited." Eve rushes to explain the offerings due to the oven issues.

I glance between them, an unwelcome comprehension flooding through me. "Where's Savannah?"

Patrick shifts in the seat next to me. "She couldn't make it."

Eve gives me an apologetic wince.

Is this what she was trying to tell me? Is this meant to be some kind of double date? Stewart and Patrick started dating soon after they both came on board two months ago. Patrick is one of the camp chefs. Stewart is a counselor specializing in psychology and they are both fresh out of college and clicked immediately.

There is no time to contemplate the situation further because Taylor reappears at the table with a tray of waters and Eve's drink, and to repeat the details of the menu to the new arrivals.

Once she takes our orders and disappears again, Patrick and Eve start telling stories about the most recent round of campers, Stewart chiming in with his own anecdotes.

Maybe I'm overanalyzing the situation. This is all fairly normal, friendly work talk. I settle back in my seat and let the conversation flow around me, contributing when I have something relevant to impart.

Working at the camp has been a new experience, friendship-wise, and not like my past jobs, since I was a contractor and worked for a variety of companies on a temporary basis.

In between the conversations, Taylor brings plates to the table, refills our drinks, and periodically stops by to ask if we need anything.

There is only one other waitress, who is taking care of people at the bar and a couple of the tables right next to it. Taylor is covering the rest of the room, which is nearly full.

I try not to stare, but it's hard not to watch her work. She's constantly in motion, moving back and forth from the kitchen. Sometimes dancing a little to the song playing from the jukebox, or singing along. Even though the restaurant is slammed, she's bright and buoyant, making customers laugh and smile. She's intoxicating.

Forcing my attention back to the conversation in front of me is a challenge.

Patrick chuckles. "We were going around the group doing introductions and she said, 'My name is Liz. And it's short for Lizard, not Elizabeth.' "

Stewart grins. "Lizard is the best. She told me her brother wants to be a marine biologist when he grows up, so she wants to be a dolphin."

We all laugh.

Glass crashing and clattering to the floor jerks my attention to the bar.

One of the patrons is looming over the other server while she wrings her hands. "You clumsy bitch!"

In a flash Taylor is there, pushing in between them, holding up her hands and facing the irate customer.

Without conscious thought, I'm on my feet, stalking in their direction.

"I'm going to need you to pay your tab and leave." Taylor's voice is low and calm.

The guy glares over her head at Vanessa. "She spilled beer on me."

The server sticks her hands on her hips. "You wouldn't keep your hands to yourself after I asked you repeatedly."

I move myself to the other side of Taylor, snagging the attention of the handsy patron and giving him my best glower.

Taylor takes a deep breath. "Sir, I witnessed you putting your hands on Vanessa and she rightfully dumped your beer in your lap."

"I didn't do—"

"Now," Taylor speaks louder, "you and your friends can pay your tab and leave, or I can call my good friend Marco. You might know him since he's the local sheriff. Did I mention he's a family friend?"

The man's expression darkens.

I clear my throat.

His bleary eyes lift to mine.

I cross my arms over my chest, daring him to do or say anything out of line so I can step in.

He swallows and his gaze dips back to Taylor's, more subdued.

"We'll leave. But we're not coming back, ever."

Taylor chuckles. "Don't threaten me with a good time."

One of his buddies drops some cash on the table and they leave, slamming the door in their wake.

After a second, the hum of conversation returns, filling the bar.

Vanessa apologizes to Taylor while wringing her hands.

"Not your fault. Go home," Taylor tells her. "Thank you for staying as long as you did and for getting a babysitter last minute."

"Are you sure? I can stay a little longer."

Taylor shakes her head. "I can cover closing duties."

Vanessa pats Taylor on the shoulder before walking away.

Taylor spins in my direction, offering me a tentative smile. "Thanks for the backup."

"Of course." I glance around at the packed bar and the waitress heading off to the back of the building. "Do you need help with anything?"

"Thank you, but I think I can handle the next ten minutes. We're done in the kitchen and since our rowdiest table is now gone, I'm doing the last call in thirty, so all that will be left other than serving is bussing tables, which can wait a minute. Thank you, though. Go have fun, enjoy your date."

I frown. "She's not my—"

But she's already walked away.

Back at the table, Stewart and Patrick are standing by the booth.

Eve looks up at me. "Are you ready to go?"

"Actually, you guys go ahead. I'll catch a ride back to camp with Taylor." I left my truck parked at the main house and rode down here with Eve.

"You sure?" Eve asks, a crease between her brows.

"Positive. I'm going to stay and help her close up. She has no one else."

Eve nods, and then leans in and puts a hand on my arm, lowering her voice. "Sorry about this whole thing. I told Patrick we're just friends, but he has it in his head that we would be good together." Her face flushes with pink. "I'll talk to him."

Relief blows through me. I'm really glad I won't have to reject Eve. We already had that uncomfortable conversation once. "It's fine. No worries."

They take off and while Taylor is hustling around the bar, I bus vacant tables.

"You don't have to do that," Taylor says as I pass by.

"I know," I call back as I'm entering the kitchen.

The sink is piled high with dishes overflowing onto the counter.

Rolling up my sleeves, I get to work.

I fill up the dishwasher and run it, leaving the remaining dishes to soak before heading back out to the bar right as Taylor rings the cowbell, letting the crowd know it's last call.

I help where I can, filling pints and water glasses, taking tabs, and giving people their receipts after Taylor rings them up.

We're passing each other behind the bar when she

stops me with a hand on my arm. Fire shoots up the limb, igniting my nerve endings.

I stop and meet her eyes, the heat of her hand on my arm like a brand.

"Thank you for staying," she says, the words soft.

"You're welcome."

After a few seconds, she moves away and we get back to work, shifting around each other behind the bar as if we've done this a million times, the movements nearly synchronized.

The next hour rushes by as people trickle out of the bar, taking the noise with them until it's just the two of us and the low strains of music coming from the jukebox.

"Will the oven be fixed by tomorrow night?" I stack a chair on a table.

"I really hope so. I'm going to call someone in the morning to come and take a look at it." She finishes wiping down the bar, tossing the dish towel into a bucket underneath.

She sighs and stretches an arm up, twisting her head to one side to work out a kink, exposing the creamy skin of her neck.

Heat rushes through me with such ferocity that I almost drop the chair in my hands. I cough to stifle the groan trying to climb up my throat. "What about the rest of the staff? Are you going to have coverage tomorrow?"

She winces. "Not tomorrow night, but hopefully by Monday we'll be back at full force."

I finish stacking the chairs and walk over to the bar opposite her, leaning my elbows on the top. "I can help out tomorrow night if you need it. I've never worked in a restaurant, but clearly, I can stack chairs like it's no one's business."

She grins, her head tilting to the kitchen. "And do dishes like a champ." Then her smile fades, and her eyes grow serious. "Thank you. Really, I appreciate your help here and earlier, when that customer got riled up."

"Of course. I didn't do anything but stand there."

"And look intimidating, which was very effective. I appreciated that you had my back. You're serious about coming back tomorrow night? Are you sure you want to spend your free time, you know." She waves a hand at the room.

"Being your bitch? Absolutely."

She throws her head back and laughs.

My chest squeezes, my heart skipping a beat and then resuming a frantic pace.

God, she's beautiful. I am so fucked.

How did I ever think I could resist her?

CHAPTER
Twelve

TAYLOR

I'm torn between immediate acceptance because I want to spend more time with him, and immediate rejection for the same reason.

"You have to let me pay you."

He shakes his head. "No way."

"If you won't take money, I can at least owe you one."

Why didn't you call?

The words are there, tickling my tongue. But the answer is obvious. He came here tonight with Eve, clearly on some kind of double date. The way they were talking, the way she touched his arm before she left . . . I shouldn't care.

Except when they walked through the door and sat together, their heads bent toward one another, her blond a bright contrast to his dark locks. They looked so good together. I thought my stomach was going to squeeze itself into knots and then leap out of my body.

But are they together? Maybe they are just close friends. The need for answers burns in my chest.

I put on a false smile. I shouldn't want him so much. He doesn't want me the same way.

He rubs the back of his head. "If you really want to help me out, I have to check out the hike to Mayberry Falls next weekend. Make sure it's hikeable for a group of teens and that the melting snowpack didn't make any of the trails impassable."

"What day next weekend?"

"Saturday. We can leave early if you need to be here for the later shift. Unless you have to work late the night before, and it's too much."

"I thought you were going with Jake."

He spreads his hands on the bar top between us, leaning in. My skin tingles at the memory of those broad fingers caressing my skin.

I imagine those same fingers touching someone else and jealousy twists my gut.

I'm not meant to be the one he touches.

Before I can second-guess the decision, the words burble out. "I'll go on the hike with you." I can figure it out. I am making the schedules here, after all.

He smiles. "Good."

I take a step back, my eyes still locked with his. "I just have to take out those." I tilt my head toward the trash stacked up at the end of the bar.

He waves a hand. "I've got it."

"Thanks. I'm going to make sure the lights are out in back."

My eyes follow as he hefts the heavy bags up, his arms flexing. How is taking out trash sexy? Who am I kidding? He would make cleaning toilets sexy.

I head toward the back rooms, welcoming the excuse to take a breath without the force of Atticus's presence and the attraction winding around us like fog.

When I finish, all the lights have been shut off except the overhead lights near the front. Atticus is waiting for me by the door, leaning with his back against the wall, his arms crossed over his chest.

I pull out my phone to kill the song playing from the jukebox, plunging us into silence.

He holds open the door for me, flicking off the lights before following me outside.

I lock it up, and then we cross the parking lot together. I take a deep breath of the night air, cool against my face after the heat of the bar. The mountain sky is showing off, the stars glittering like a sparkling blanket over our heads.

We reach the Jeep and Atticus turns to me. "Do you want me to drive?"

"That would be great." I toss him the keys.

It's only a few minutes to home, but I'm exhausted. I could use a second to relax, decompress, and not think about anything. I climb into the passenger seat and immediately plug my phone in. "Is this okay?"

"Of course."

"Thanks. Music helps me decompress. Or peps me up, when I need that. Or helps me think."

"It's an all-inclusive emotion enhancer."

"That is the truth." I push some buttons until Bob Marley's "Three Little Birds" plays through the speakers.

While Atticus reverses out of the parking spot, I shut my eyes and lean back in the seat.

There's something about a reggae beat that's relaxing. The music reminds me of summers at the lake and relaxing with the sun beating down on my body with nothing to worry about except putting on more sunscreen and waking up for lunch.

Atticus, bless him, isn't compelled to fill the space with chatter. It's like he understands me. Kind of like how he stood behind me and offered support without intervening when I had to deal with those asshole customers. It's like he knows what I need better than I do.

Not to mention how he knows my body better than I do.

Warmth pools low in my belly, ready for a repeat.

But my brain cuts through the arousal. *He didn't call.*

He was out tonight, with Eve.

When the vehicle rolls to a stop, I blink my eyes open and shift my head to look at Atticus. I'm not ready to leave yet. It's comfortable in this space with him, despite it all. And I need answers. Why didn't he call? Is it because of Eve, or is there something else?

Atticus angles toward me, his head back against the headrest, his eyes warm on mine. "Tired?"

"Exhausted. So exhausted, I don't think I can move from this spot. Maybe I'll sleep here."

He chuckles. "You had a long night. Do you regret agreeing to manage Veronica's while she's away?"

I mimic his posture, aiming my body in his direction. "Honestly, I enjoyed tonight more than I thought I would."

"Even with the asshole?"

"Yeah. Even then. It was sort of satisfying to solve difficult problems, you know? It made it more exciting." I wasn't bored, that's for sure. Boredom leads to thinking too much, dwelling too much on things I can't change, thinking about the past and everything that drove me away from Whitby in the first place.

"But not as exciting as a music festival?"

I grin. "Adding live music would make it almost perfect. Everything is better with music."

His eyes fix on mine with genuine curiosity. "Why? Other than the emotion-enhancing abilities."

"It's hard to explain. Experiencing music with other people is like"—I wave a hand, searching for the words —"it's collective effervescence. That feeling you get when you're experiencing something amazing with a group of people. It's almost like transcendence. It's probably the same thing people feel in church or watching a beloved football team score a touchdown with a million other fans, cheering together. There's a synchrony to our bodies, our thoughts, our feelings."

His gaze goes thoughtful. "You should bring the music here."

I blink. "What?"

"Finley told me how you helped Luke and Mindy by bringing Laila here. How you've made all these connections from the festivals. You could do that for yourself, bring artists to play here, at Veronica's."

I stare at him. The idea worms its way into my mind, taking root. "Oh, I couldn't."

His brows lift. "Why not?"

My mind immediately spins through what it would take to make it happen.

It would be a lot of work. I wouldn't even know where to start.

Veronica would have to be okay with it. Who would I even ask to come here to play? What about the audience? Could I get some friends and influencers to show up and spread the word? To what end, though?

I won't be here long enough to plan anything major or long-term.

Flustered, I lift my hands. "I don't know. I'm leaving soon."

I'm happy with my life the way it is. I'm free. I'm not beholden to anyone or anything.

A little voice squeaks in the back of my mind: *Is that true, or am I actually beholden to my need to always run?*

I shove the voice away. "It's not possible."

The words are like a wet blanket dropped on top of a cozy fire.

His face falls. "Right. I get it." He turns away, plucking the keys from the ignition.

I open my palm and he drops them, the distance between us lengthening even though we haven't exited the car.

Right.

I push open the door and get out but my feet stick to the ground. I can't go into the house yet, not without knowing.

"Have a good night." Atticus steps around me, heading for his truck.

"Is Eve the reason why you didn't call?" The words escape, leaping out of my mouth before I can hold them back.

Atticus halts and then turns around to face me, stepping closer until we're only a foot apart. The porch light illuminates half of his face, his eyes dark and unreadable. "No. Eve and I are friends."

I wrap my arms around myself, bracing for an answer to the question I can't hold back any longer. "Then why didn't you call?"

His gaze dips to the ground between us before lifting again to meet my eyes. "You said it yourself, you're leaving."

I blink. "Isn't that exactly what makes a fling ideal?"

He rubs the back of his head. "It's just that, I don't know if I'm exactly the flinging type." He shoves his hands into his pockets.

Shame crashes through me. *Oh shit.* Here I am, throwing myself at him constantly. He probably thinks

I'm a total tramp. No wonder he didn't call. "Oh. I . . . I'm sorry."

He takes quick steps toward me, his head shaking. "No, it's not your fault. It's not anything you did." He winces. "It sounds so lame, 'it's not you, it's me,' but the truth is," he swallows, "if we started something, I'm afraid I would want more than a fling. But I don't blame you or judge you for wanting a fling."

My mouth pops open in surprise. "Oh."

"It isn't fair to put you in that position. You aren't responsible for my emotions. So when I say it's not you, I mean it. You've been nothing but honest with me."

I stare at him. It shouldn't be so attractive, this blunt admission that if we continue a physical relationship, his feelings might get involved.

Any other guy telling me this kind of line, I'd bolt for the hills.

With Atticus, though, it's different. He's not like other guys I've been involved with. They all knew the score and were one hundred percent down for a temporary arrangement.

Atticus is smart, kind, caring, and brutally honest, even if it renders him vulnerable. He's the gawky teen who saw a broken girl and drove her home, no questions asked when we were seventeen. He's the rugged man who gave me shelter in a storm and more pleasure than my last four lovers combined.

Shit.

Maybe he's right. A fling would be a bad idea.

The ever-present hum of tension urging me to flee is

suddenly pushing me to do something else entirely. Something that involves hauling Atticus somewhere private and then spending excessive amounts of time exploring this spark.

The depth of the desire crackling between us stretches, immense and terrifying.

I duck my head, staring at the ground. "Thank you, for being honest. I'm sorry."

"You have no reason to be sorry."

I lift my head, meeting his eyes. Unwilling to accept that this is it, that we're just going to go about our lives like there's nothing between us. "Friends." The word pops out of my mouth without forethought. "We can be friends. Right?"

He rocks back on his heels. "Yeah. Friends. Absolutely."

We can be friends. Friends is good. Friends is better, for both of us.

I can always use a friend.

Then why is my heart heavy with loss?

"Sounds like you were put through the wringer and you handled it like a champ." Veronica's raspy chuckle echoes over the speakerphone. "Vanessa called me yesterday. She said you were impressive at thinking on your feet."

"There were a few fires," I mutter, shuffling through the paperwork on the desk. "Everything has been taken care of. Gloria will be back tonight, and the stove is in working order."

It only needed a new heating element, which was thankfully cheap. I pick up the invoice I'd been searching for from the produce supplier and key the info into the accounting program opened on the computer. "And you'll be back tomorrow night?"

The ensuing silence goes on a little too long. Did I lose her?

"Veronica?"

She clears her throat. "About that. Rachel is having some complications and they're putting her on bed rest."

"Oh no." My fingers still on the keyboard. "Is she okay? Is the baby okay?"

"The baby is fine, and Rachel is hanging in there. She needs to stay off her feet as much as possible until the baby comes so I need to extend my stay here a bit longer than we thought. Are you okay with continuing to take care of things there? I can search for a replacement if not."

"I can stay on longer, of course," I say. Words that used to give me anxious jitters, and yet they emerge so easily.

"I know it's not ideal, but you're staying for at least another month, right? And I'll keep paying you more for the extra work I know you're doing, so by the time I get back, you'll have enough for your bus."

Right. The bus. So I can leave. Go about my business as usual.

"Can I bring some musical acts here?" The words blurt out of my mouth as if they've been poised and waiting the past two days to be set free. Ever since Atticus mentioned the idea, it's been nudging at me, and I've been unable to shake it.

The shocked silence emanating from the speaker is nearly palpable. "Really?"

"I was thinking, just a couple gigs here and there. Very chill."

But like with Luke's show, I could invite producers and influencers, and get the buzz going for some lesser-known acts.

I squirm in the chair, making it squeak. "It's just a possibility. Forget it. It's a bad idea."

"Now wait a minute. It's a good idea."

I swallow. "I don't know."

"No, it's perfect." Veronica's voice is eager. "Taylor, I insist you do it. You have my blessing. Hell, you have free rein to do whatever you like as long as you don't burn the place down." She chuckles.

A rush of excitement blows through me, along with nerves and anticipation, the ache to accomplish some-thing, something good, something to focus on.

We chat about some other bar business before hanging up, my mind buzzing from all the ideas, thoughts, and actions I need to take.

Other than finding musicians and industry peeps and getting them to come out to the middle of nowhere, I have to consider the space and if I want to use it like they did with Luke, or if we should do an outdoor stage. After all, it is June, and the weather has been perfect. Veronica's property is huge, extending back into the trees and to either side, probably about twenty acres.

But the area directly around the bar could use a bit of cleaning up. There is a junked-out car gathering rust, a moldy sofa with missing cushions, and an old porcelain clawfoot tub nestled under a maple tree.

I might be able to do something creative with some of it, like the old bathtub out there.

Hmm.

My phone dings.

> I have a solid lead for you. Not too far from your hometown. It's in PA.
> Call me.

It's the PI, Georgia. Pennsylvania? Did Mom leave us to end up one state away?

I pick up my phone and push on Georgia's name.

She answers after two rings.

"Tell me."

CHAPTER
Thirteen

TAYLOR

I'm sitting on the porch swing, gently rocking back and forth, enjoying my coffee when Atticus pulls up in his truck.

The sun has just crested the mountains, throwing a faint gold sheen over every surface. Atticus hops out of the truck, the rising sun illuminating the scruff on his jaw and the way his sweater hugs his broad shoulders.

Friends. Just friends. Right.

The past week has been a blur of work, work, and even more work. I don't think I've ever spent so many hours in an office voluntarily. My days have been stuffed full of paperwork and phone calls, trying to connect to musicians and influencers while working the bar, and it hasn't been as much of a nightmare as I might have expected. As a matter of fact, it's been fun.

I stand and greet Atticus at the bottom of the steps. "Hey."

His mouth curves up, his eyes downcast, a faint flush tinging his cheeks. "Hi."

Could he be any cuter? I squash down all the unsatisfied lust that's been a relentless thrum in my veins for days.

Ugh.

Once we hit the road, he hands me the cord to plug in my phone, keeping one hand on the wheel.

"Thanks." I fill the truck with String Cheese Incident.

"So tell me about this trail and what I can expect on this hike. What's our plan?"

He adjusts the rearview mirror before glancing over at me. "We'll go slow. I need to time how long it will take with a group. It's a survival camp, so I need to check out what's growing up there right now, what's in bloom and edible and anything poisonous, along with where they can look for shelter, what to do if they encounter a bear, that kind of thing."

"I'm sorry did you say *bear*? Do you think we'll see one? Will it eat us?"

He chuckles. "Even seeing one is unlikely. This region has black bears, but they are active mostly late at night and early morning. If any are around, we would probably scare them away with our noise before they get too close."

I purse my lips and lift a hand. "Probably?"

"Don't worry, you don't have to outrun the bear, you just need to outrun me."

A surprised laugh bursts out of me and I rub my chin. "How often do you run?"

"Never, if I can help it."

"So you're telling me I have a chance?"

His gaze travels down my face to my legs. "I have a longer stride, and I spend a lot of my time hiking. But you seem fit enough to have a sporting chance." His eyes go hot.

My mouth drops open. Is he . . . flirting with me?

Friends don't stare like they want to devour each other.

Before I can respond, he's parking next to an old red Subaru, the only other car in the lot.

We stretch for a couple minutes, and then I follow him up a set of stone steps, following the signs to the trail.

The breeze tickles the trees rustling the leaves over our heads. Birds chirp in the distance, their calls increasing in volume as we head up the path.

It's too narrow for us to walk side by side, but Atticus keeps the pace slow and steady, and the silence is comfortable. Every now and again, I catch a whiff of his deodorant, mixed with sunscreen, pine, and fresh air.

I jump over a large rock in the center of the path. "How far are we going?"

"Just a few miles. Here." He crouches down, pulling a leaf from a spindly, white-flowered plant and crushing it with his fingers. He sniffs it, then hands it to me.

Our fingers brush, and I do my best to subdue the rush of yearning incited by the small movement.

Friends.

I take a small taste and then my gaze flies to his in surprise. "Garlicky."

"It's garlic mustard." He stands, wiping his hands on his pants, and grins at me. "Come on, there's more."

I follow and he stops occasionally to show me various edible plants. His eyes are bright, his face animated, and his enthusiasm is palpable.

He loves this.

I love that I get to experience it with him.

He plucks some bright green leaves from the forest floor that look like clover and hands me a pinch. "Wood sorrel."

I pop a small leaf in my mouth. "Sort of lemony."

"It's good in salads."

When we're hiking up the trail again, I ask, "So, what do I do if I'm lost in the woods and you aren't around? How can I tell if something is poisonous?"

"There is a universal edibility test. In general, though, you want to stay away from plants with milky sap, fine hairs, or shiny, waxy leaves. Green and white berries are usually signs of an inedible plant." He holds back an overgrown branch for me to pass through ahead of him. "If you still aren't sure," he continues, "you can do a skin contact test. Rub it against the inside of your elbow, or your lips. If there's no burning, put it in your mouth and then spit it out."

"Huh." I twist my head to look at him over my shoulder. "Spitting isn't something most guys have recommended to me."

He stops walking, throws back his head, and laughs, the sound echoing around us.

I turn around fully to take him in.

He's gorgeous like this. Surrounded by greenery, happy, smiling at me with warm eyes. "Now I see where Jake gets it from."

I bite my lip. "You love my sick sense of humor."

"You know, heaven help me, but I do." He searches my face, his smile dropping. His head dips and he clears his throat. "We only have another hour or so."

Right.

Friends. The most annoying word ever invented.

I motion for him to lead the way. "So what made you get interested in hiking and eating plants and all this?"

"I used to hike a lot with my dad. He was really into foraging. He loved mushroom hunting." His tone turns wistful. "He started taking me with him when I was around seven."

I step around a log jutting halfway into the path. "What about your cousins, or Paul and Moira? Do they hike or anything?"

"I'm not sure. Paul and Moira are into golf. My cousins like water sports."

"You should take them out here too, show them how to forage."

He shrugs. "Maybe."

We walk in silence for a few minutes before he speaks again. "I think it's hard sometimes for my family to be around me."

Surprise halts me in my tracks and then I have to speed walk to catch up to him. "Why would that be? Other than making me eat weeds, you're not too bad."

He chuckles, and then we walk in silence.

I think maybe we've left that question back in the dirt where it will linger forever, but then he speaks. "When I first came to Whitby, I was a mess."

"Of course you were." I know that better than most. "You lost your parents. You were only sixteen."

"Yeah but . . . I don't know, it's been over ten years now and I still feel separate somehow. Like I'm part of the family, but not."

Understanding whispers through me. The connection already taut between us hooks into my stomach and tugs. "I feel that way too, sometimes."

"Seriously? But your family is so . . . " He waves a hand in the air, searching for the words.

"Loud. Obnoxious. Major crap-talkers."

A smile tugs at the corner of his mouth. "Yes, but you're all so close with each other."

"We are, but there is tension sometimes too."

"You mean, like with Mindy."

"Yeah. Like with Mindy." Which I do not want to talk

about. "But it's more than that. Mindy and Finley are only a year apart, so they've always been tight. Piper and Mindy are close too, even though Piper is three years younger than her. They even lived together recently, before Piper moved in with Oliver. Then there's me. Smack dab in the middle of all my siblings." The odd one out. The one who hasn't done anything with her life.

He stops and turns to face me, eyes locking with mine. "Like you're a part of something, but not."

"Yes. Exactly."

We stare at each other, the seconds stretching between us until he spins around and continues walking. "We're almost to the stopping point."

I find my voice. "Okay."

After a few more minutes, he glances over his shoulder. "Did you know Finley and Jake got me gifts for Christmas?"

"Really? Didn't Finley invite you at the very last minute? They couldn't have had time to buy anything. What did they get you?"

"Jake gave me a hammer. A used one. It has paint splatters on it. He carved my initials into it. Well, one of my initials. He couldn't remember my last name so there's just a poorly carved A on the handle." He chuckles.

I shake my head. "That tracks. What did Finley get you? I'm sure it was better than a hammer."

"She got me a succulent. She painted on the pot, 'I wet my plants.' "

Laughter breaks out of me. "Oh, Finley. She's such a

mom. On my tenth birthday I got in a fight with my best friend, Lily, who was supposed to come over that night for a sleepover."

"I don't remember a Lily at Whitby High."

I sidle around a scraggly bush growing into the path. "She moved away during middle school. Anyway, I was super upset and Finley threw together this whole thing with my sisters. She and Mindy made a big old fort with pillows and blankets in the living room, covered it in Christmas lights, and let me eat cake for dinner."

"Your parents didn't mind?"

"Dad took Jake to Veronica's. Mom hasn't been around since I was two. I don't remember anything about her."

The urge to spill the truth to him, to tell him how I've been searching for Mom, tickles in my throat. But I haven't told anyone. Is it weird he's the one person I want to share with?

He stops suddenly, sticking out his hand to halt me in my tracks.

"What is it?" I whisper.

My ears prickle. About thirty feet up the trail, a bush rustles, the leaves shaking and shivering.

A deep growl rumbles through the air.

Oh, shit.

My mouth goes dry.

Atticus steps further in front of me, blocking me from whatever is up ahead.

Okay, so the protectiveness is kind of hot.

I grab his hand.

His fingers squeeze mine.

I peek around Atticus, trying to get an idea of what's up ahead.

Is it a bear? Is it going to eat us? This is it. We're going to die. We're going to get eaten by a bear and die.

The headline will read *local hippie and hot botanist eaten by wild bears*. My obituary will be blank because what the hell have I done with my life to this point? Nothing.

Except listen to some really great music and fail to get the hot botanist into bed.

I've done nothing of true value. I haven't helped anyone, I've only run away from things.

All of these thoughts form and then fly away as the bushes part.

My heart pounds so loud, my vision blurs and I have to blink to take in the creature. Black and white and gray fur, beady eyes . . . whiskers?

It's a goddamn raccoon.

My grip on Atticus eases and a shaky laugh tumbles out of my mouth.

Okay, so it's the biggest raccoon I've ever seen, sure, but it's so cute, the little black nose twitching while he wiggles his little human-shaped hands in the air.

The raccoon ambles toward us, rearing up on its hind legs.

"Is it supposed to be doing that?"

Atticus's throat bobs as he swallows. Is he scared?

He's six four and at least two hundred pounds. The raccoon is smaller than a golden retriever.

He whispers to me out the side of his mouth. "Maybe it's a female protecting her young. Or maybe it has rabies."

Rabies? "If it bites us, will we die?" The words are a strangled hiss. The only thing I know about animals with rabies comes from *Old Yeller*.

Jake begged and begged to watch the old movie when he was six because Dad made a comment about how it traumatized him as a kid. I think Jake thought it was some kind of horror movie. When the dog got rabies and died in the end, Aria cried for three days straight.

Because of course she had to watch it if Jake wanted to.

Why am I thinking about this?

The raccoon bares its teeth and snarls, the sound low and menacing.

We are so going to die.

"What do we do?" I ask.

"Back away slowly."

He takes a step and I take it with him, our hands gripped together.

The raccoon takes running steps in our direction and then stops again.

I squeak in alarm. "It's following us."

"We need to move slowly and stay calm." His voice is a low, soothing rumble.

The raccoon opens its mouth and shrieks, the sound reverberating through me.

I jump, grabbing at Atticus with my other hand. "It's going to kill us. It's a homicidal raccoon."

"Turn around and walk back down the trail. Slowly. No sudden moves."

It's a testament to my trust in Atticus, the bone-deep knowledge that he would die before letting anything happen to me, that allows me to follow his directions. I wrench my eyes away from the raccoon, turning around and taking careful steps back down the path. We move back to back, our hands still linked, Atticus walking backward behind me with shuffling steps.

After interminable heart-thumping minutes, Atticus finally speaks. "Okay, we're good. It's gone."

All the gathering stress whooshes out of my body, leaving me lightheaded. My heart races, vibrating against my rib cage. My breath saws in and out like I ran a marathon instead of walking at a snail's pace for two hundred yards.

"We almost got ravaged by a feral raccoon," I say slowly, using the back of my arm to wipe sweat from my brow.

A giggle bursts out of me and I smack a hand over my mouth.

But it's too late. Atticus's shoulders shake and we double over, my hand still gripped in his.

"You should have seen your face," I tell him through fits of laughter.

"Me? You were so scared you almost squeezed my hand off," he says, wiping his eyes.

"You're still squeezing my hand off." I look down at our linked hands.

His eyes drop too, both of us staring down where our fingers are joined.

Awareness reverberates out from that point of connection, spreading warmth through my body, the heat coiling low in my stomach.

Maybe it's the sudden release of tension and almost dying at the tiny hands of an evil raccoon, maybe it's because Atticus is the sexiest, sweetest, most compelling man I've ever met, but all I can think about is his lips on mine, his body covering me.

Our eyes lock.

His gaze is a reflection of the turmoil pounding through me, hot, conflicted, searching for permission.

"Taylor—" he starts, his tone tortured.

"I know." I step into him, lifting up on my toes and weaving my fingers into the thick strands of his hair.

His head dips and then his mouth clashes against mine.

CHAPTER

Fourteen

ATTICUS

The only thing that exists is the point where our skin meets. The rest of the world fades away under the onslaught of her touch, the heat of her hand in my hair, the smell of her skin, a mixture of soap and sweat and sweetness.

Then her lips part, her tongue brushes against mine and the motion nearly brings me to my knees.

I wouldn't hesitate to actually get on my knees for her, even with the rocks and dirt and pine needles covering the ground underneath us. I can think of a lot of things I could do right now on my knees.

The taste of her on my tongue is a memory I've returned to time and time again since December.

My entire body jolts to life.

My fingers skate down her back, stopping just

before the curve of her ass. I grip her hips, luxuriating in the feel of her, *finally*. Her body is perfectly formed for my hands.

She shifts closer, her breasts pressing against my chest, her hips tilting against mine.

It was inevitable that I would give in to this attraction between us. I don't know why I fought against it so hard.

"I need you," she says against my mouth.

"Yes."

"I know you didn't want a fling, but maybe we just need to get it out of our systems, you know? And then maybe being around each other won't be so," she swallows, "so . . ."

"Compulsive?"

"Yes."

"Right."

One time won't be enough. I already know it; it's written in my bones. Hell, a hundred might not be enough, but I'll go with it for now, and maybe I can change her mind later. Not that I would ask her to change her life, but maybe adjust it enough to make space for me.

My thumb brushes over the fluttering pulse in her neck, the skin silky smooth under my fingers. I can't resist her. Never could. "Yes," I say.

Her eyes brighten.

"But not here," I add.

"What?" She stretches up, nipping at my jawline with gentle teeth. "Why?"

"The first time I sink inside you it's not going to be in the dirt, Taylor."

She pulls back, her hands running down my arms and her eyes tracking the movement. "How far are we from the truck?"

I shake my head, chuckling. "Not in my truck either."

"Why not?" She juts her chin out, mouth curving into a displeased frown.

I chuckle, brushing my thumb over her plump bottom lip, swollen from my mouth. The thought fills me with more satisfaction than I care to admit. "No one's at my house right now."

Her eyes widen, her frown curving into a smile. "What about finishing the hike?"

"We were nearly finished. I have enough for Finley."

"We better hurry then." She's already tugging on my hand, heading back down the path.

The hike back down does nothing to cool the simmering need burning through my blood, not even a degree.

We make it to the truck in record time, out of breath from the exertions of our hike and the insistent craving pulsing between us.

For the first time, Taylor doesn't bother with music. She sits on her hands while I drive, my fingers clenched around the steering wheel to keep them from reaching for her. The ride is silent except for the hum of the tires on the pavement and our mingled breathing.

It takes everything in me to concentrate on the road

and not on pulling over and taking her right here, right now.

By the time we pull up in front of my house, I'm vibrating with desire. I barely manage to get the truck in park before jumping out of the vehicle.

I've taken three steps when Taylor's door bangs shut and then she's there, her arms winding around me.

"Jump," I tell her.

With zero hesitation, she complies, leaping up and wrapping her legs around me. I clutch her tightly, cupping her ass in both hands, lifting her high enough that our mouths are lined up.

Taylor throws herself into the kiss, *into me* like she does everything else, with absolute abandon.

I get lost in sensations, in the slide of her tongue against mine, the desperate grip of her hands on my shoulders, the taste of her mouth and the heady scent of her skin filling my lungs.

We kiss until the yearning overwhelms every other thought except I need to be inside Taylor more than I need air. I pull my mouth away far enough to ensure we don't trip while I jog up the porch steps. Taylor's lips trace down the column of my throat and I groan.

The door hinders our progress while I make fumbling attempts to punch in the code. Once we make it inside, I kick the door shut behind me.

Taylor removes her mouth from my neck long enough to say, "Couch is right there."

"We need more space to do this properly."

She shivers in my arms. "I can't wait to see what *properly* entails."

Without another word, I carry her into my room and toss her on the bed.

She bounces, eyes sparkling, her face flushed and her laughter husky. She tugs off her shoes and chucks them over the side of the bed. Her hair is wild around her face.

I want to wrap the strands around my fingers while I take her slowly, then quickly, over and over again.

Her eyes rake over me, coming to an abrupt halt at the bulge pressing against the zipper of my pants.

I rip my sweater over my head, and then my shirt.

Her eyes stay locked on my body as she removes the top half of her clothes, tossing them onto the floor.

Her chest heaves up and down, breath going ragged as she reaches behind her and unclasps her bra.

She tosses it to the side. Light filters in through the curtains, caressing her skin in a midday glow.

"Damn, but you're perfect." The words are low, fervent. I shove my pants down to the floor, my briefs coming off with them, and I bend over to yank my feet from the hiking boots.

When I stand up again, her gaze sharpens on my throbbing erection. "I want that," her voice is husky with the same ache pounding through me.

I lean forward to pull her shorts off before crawling up the bed and coming over top of her.

Then we're kissing again, her mouth meeting mine with reckless urgency.

Her breasts rub against my chest and my cock jerks against the soft skin of her belly. *Holy shit.* Her flesh rubbing against mine is incredible. Indescribable.

This is going to be over before I can get inside her.

I adjust my hips to slide the crown of my cock against her deliciously wet folds and we both groan, breaking the connection of our mouths.

"Do you have a condom?" she whispers.

The words don't immediately register in my lust-addled brain.

"Condom?" I repeat, swallowing hard, forcing my sluggish mind to work out the meaning of the word.

Her eyes search mine. "I'm on the pill and I was tested last year. I haven't been with anyone else in a while. Not since before Christmas. Way before Christmas."

It takes a full minute for me to sort out the statements. She hasn't been with anyone else. Not since the last time we . . . my cock grows impossibly harder.

"Same," I manage to get out.

"So you're okay with proceeding, no condom?"

I nod.

"Thank the gods," she breathes. She shifts underneath me, reaching between us.

When her hand wraps around me, stars explode across my vision.

I take a deep breath. "Holy shit."

She smiles and adjusts me so I'm right at her entrance, poised and waiting.

I swallow, hard. "I've never done this before."

She blinks up at me, confusion marring her brow. "Wait. Are you a . . . virgin?"

"What? No. No, I mean, I've done *this* before, but never without a condom."

She puts her hands over her face, laughing, before shoving me playfully on the shoulder. "I was really freaked out for a second, but also kinda turned on."

I quirk my brow at her. "Really?"

She nods, eyes darkening with renewed lust. "We could have done this whole teacher-student thing. I could show you exactly what I like and how I like it."

Unable to help myself, I thrust a little, the head of my cock entering her by an inch.

Her breath catches in her throat.

"We could still do a whole student-teacher thing." I dip my head into the space between her neck, chuckling against her skin. "We could take turns."

"I want to be teacher first." Her fingers trail up and down my spine as the humor mixes with the ever-present heat between us, blossoming like a morning glory under the first rays of sun.

I pull back to meet her eyes as I slide in another inch.

My mind blanks. She's perfect. Tight, hot, wet, and sweet. I never want to leave.

Pure bliss. This is heaven. And also not going to last long at all. I'll be lucky if I can get all the way inside her without spilling.

I take a deep breath and shut my eyes while going

through the seven major tracheophyte divisions in my head before pushing forward another inch.

"Atticus."

Taylor's soft voice prompts me to open my eyes.

She bites her swollen bottom lip. "I've never done this before either. Not like this."

This.

I'm not alone in this. It isn't just me, treading around this thing between us. It's expansive. Daunting. Unfathomable.

Keeping our eyes locked, I drive inside her to the hilt.

Her mouth parts and for a second we stare at each other. Her eyes are soft, the pupils wide with arousal, cheeks flushed with heat.

I give her a second to adjust to the sensations, my fingers delving into her hair, tugging the hair tie off. Then I wrap a long, silky strand around my wrist.

I move, pulling out slowly, and then thrusting back in.

She gasps.

This could never be casual.

A sliver of panic worms its way into my heart, piercing my chest.

She's still leaving. She won't stay.

I can't keep her.

Banishing thoughts of the future in favor of this much more enjoyable moment, I lower my head to press my lips to hers.

I will enjoy her while I can.

I will savor every moment, every touch. The way her hands grip my back, trailing down to clutch my ass and urge me on, the way her breasts rub against my chest as I thrust into her body.

I angle my hips so I can grind against her clit with each forward plunge.

My spine tingles. It's too much. Too good. I have to hold off until she comes, and from the wetness and fluttering of her muscles around my shaft, she's getting there sooner rather than later.

Please be sooner.

A minute of ecstasy later, I can't hold back any longer.

No mind tricks can stop my body from exploding with pleasure. My orgasm builds and erupts and I cry out.

As soon as I pulse inside her, she follows me over the edge, her inner muscles contracting around me.

When the shudders subside, I roll and tug Taylor with me, draping her boneless, limp form across my chest.

I press a kiss to her sweaty brow and try to calm my racing body, try to figure out how my world has suddenly splintered and reformed around the Taylor-size shape in my heart.

Her legs tangle with mine, her fingers tracing small, ticklish circles on my skin.

One of my hands toys with the silky dark strands of her hair.

The sun angles into the room, through the blinds, casting golden lines over the curves of Taylor's body.

My mind is hazy. Is there something else we're supposed to be doing?

It's hard to think too much, to care about anything other than Taylor's soft warmth pressed into my side.

I only know one thing for certain. This is more than sex. More than just getting it out of our systems. She's like a comet striking the surface of the earth and just as life altering.

Minutes pass and then she lifts up, propping her chin on her hands to look into my face.

I'm still playing with her hair, relishing the fact that I get to. "Hey."

Her responding grin is blinding. I can't breathe for a full three seconds.

"That was incredible." Her gaze drops, dark lashes casting shadows on her cheeks. "Do you think—I mean, I know we said it was a one-time thing. Just to get it out of our systems, but what if we extended that whole one-time thing a smidge?"

Hell yes. Extend it to infinity.

But I can't say that. If I tell her how the thought of letting her go shreds me up, she'll leave a Taylor-shaped ring of smoke in her rush to escape.

"Extending sounds good," I manage.

"We are still friends. But we are friends who . . . do other things." Her hand traces a path down my stomach, stopping on my lower abs.

I instantly harden.

Friends is impossible. Friends is never going to happen. I want her too much to ever go back to something as tedious as *friends*.

But what other option is there? She's leaving. I want her however I can get her. I can't say no, not now, not ever.

I swallow. "Friends. Who do other things," I confirm. "And we don't do these other things with any other friends." I duck my head to her neck, sucking gently on the spot below her ear.

Her breathing falters. "Yes." The word is hissed through her teeth.

If I'm agreeing to this heartbreak, which is inevitable, I refuse to share. My lips follow a path down to her collarbone, nipping softly.

She groans and shifts against me. "Can we do some of those other things now?"

Triumphant, I grin against her skin. "We can do them whenever you want."

CHAPTER
Fifteen

Atticus's chest is the best pillow in the world. Maybe a little firmer than what I'm used to, but his skin is like brushed satin over smooth steel and the beat of his heart in my ear is more soothing than a Gregorian chant.

I'm half dozing, enjoying the feel of his warm skin against mine, when a distant series of pings tugs me from the threshold of sleep.

I jerk up to a seat. My phone. *Finley*. Shit.

The sun's rays slanting through the window are angled lower than they were just a minute ago. Maybe it was a couple of hours ago.

I shift away from Atticus's warmth. His hand tightens around me, luring me back, his eyes still closed. I give in for a few blissful seconds and then my phone pings again.

"I think that's Finley," I say, my voice low.

His drowsy, soft eyes meet mine and then sharpen. "Finley?"

Realization dawns, washing over his face and leaving a flush in its wake.

"We never called to check in." He scrubs a hand over his face. "I think I left my cell in the truck."

I scramble out of bed, plucking my shorts off the ground and finding my phone in the pocket.

Five missed calls and eight texts.

The phone rings in my hand and I swipe my finger across the screen to answer.

"Finley, hey." I sit on the edge of the bed, facing Atticus, still sprawled in the center.

She blows out a noisy breath. "Taylor, holy hell, I thought you were lying in a ditch somewhere, or stung by killer bees, or choked on red gummy bears and dead."

"Red gummy bears? That's oddly specific."

"I've been having really weird dreams and red gummies are delicious. Now where are you?"

I bite my lip and meet Atticus's eyes, before my gaze trails over the rest of him.

He rolls to his side, propping his head on a hand, the sheet draped over his hips leaving very little to the imagination.

That chest. Those arms. His mouth, dark pink and puffy from kissing me.

Heat rushes through my body, head to toe, despite the fact that we've spent the past I-don't-even-know-how-many hours bringing each other to orgasm over and over. I lost count after four, but one look, one glance at his naked body and I'm ready all over again.

It's never been like this with anyone else.

Of course no one else has been able to translate my body like a book written in a language only he can read.

I shove the horny thoughts to the side and focus on the conversation at hand. Finley. I can't be having sexy thoughts while I'm talking to my sister and I have to explain our whereabouts for the past six hours without telling her that I'm naked with her employee.

"We're at Atticus's house." When prevaricating, it's always best to stick as close to the truth as possible.

Also find ways to delay for time to think of something.

"What are you doing there?"

I grimace at Atticus.

He shrugs.

Unhelpful.

"Our hike took a little longer than we anticipated. We had a little incident with a raccoon up on the trail."

"Oh no. Are you okay? I've had run-ins with those sneaky little buggers on the property." She sounds almost nostalgic about it.

"This one was not little. And it had rabies. Or babies. It was a babies-rabies-riddled raccoon."

Atticus shakes his head, laughing quietly.

Finley's voice goes dreamy. "Right after we first met,

Archer saved me from a raccoon that had taken up residence in one of the cabins. That's when I knew he was a keeper."

Still pressing the phone to my ear, I glance up and lock eyes with Atticus.

He smiles and it's like a punch to the chest.

I bite my lip, looking away. "Anyway, uh, we headed back down the mountain and then stopped here because Atticus forgot his phone." I wink at him. That will cover any calls he missed from Finley. I'm a lying genius. "We haven't eaten anything except granola bars and trail food all day, so we're going to grab something to eat before I come home. I might need to run by Veronica's too." Just in case I need to have him one extra time.

He slides over the bed toward me, running his lips over the outside of my thigh, causing tingles to race over the surface of my skin.

"You want to eat with us? Archer is making fried chicken."

"Actually, Atticus already started cooking."

His finger, inching up my inner thigh halts halfway there. His brows lift. "Cooking?" he mouths.

"Okay. Tell Atticus to give me a briefing of the hike, including any potential raccoon threats we need to worry about, in the morning."

"I'll let him know."

We hang up and I toss my phone into the pile of clothes on the floor where it lands with a soft thunk.

Atticus wraps his arms around my waist, kissing the curve of my side.

"That tickles."

In response, he blows a raspberry into the same spot and the giggle escalates into laughter.

He hauls my leg toward him. I slide onto my back and then he crawls up and over me, his hands on either side of my head and his hips pressing against mine, his hardness pushing between my legs.

He's insatiable.

But so am I.

I am going to be sore tomorrow, but there's no way I'm going to tell him to stop.

His eyes search mine. "You don't want your family to know about us?"

I put a hand on his cheek, reading the insecurity in his expression, in the careful lilt of his words. "I'm just trying to save us both from the fallout. I don't want to make things weird for you when I'm gone. Besides, they would be so obnoxious if they knew anything was going on between us."

He nods slowly, his gaze dipping down my body, masking a flash of hurt. "No. You're right. It's best if we keep things just between us."

The thought of causing Atticus even an iota of pain tears me up. But before I can say anything, talk it out with him, his mouth traces a fiery path down my chest, lingering over my sensitive nipples, the scruff of his jaw abrading my skin in the most delicious way.

"Since you mentioned eating, I am hungry." His

head lifts from my breasts. "How much time do we have?"

I can barely speak. What is time? I don't even care. "Lots. Lots of time."

"Good." Then he moves lower and proceeds to show me how he is very hungry indeed.

CHAPTER
Sixteen

TAYLOR

"I'm booking solo acts right now, and you would be perfect." I'm in Veronica's office, my phone pressed to my ear. The same position I've spent most of my days lately, eyeballing the dry erase calendar I stuck on the wall. It's where I've been keeping track of the employees' schedules along with the live music dates and times.

"I don't know, Taylor, do you think it would be worth it? Whitby is such a small venue." Derek is a soulful singer, absolutely amazing once you get him onstage, but a hot mess behind the scenes. I met him at a dive bar in New Orleans three years ago. He was having a full-blown panic attack in a back alley, and I convinced him to get on the stage and kill it. And he did. We've been friends ever since.

He has a midsize but loyal fanbase that grows daily, and he's done some smaller festivals, like Firefly and High Sierra.

"I've confirmed A.J. Fullerton will be here both nights and I know what he likes. He is going to love you. I also invited Caroline Gray." A.J. is a producer and Caroline is an influencer with almost a million followers.

At Derek's continued silence, I add, "Plus I'm offering a cut of alcohol sales for the night. I'm only scheduling for the next two weekends. Friday and Saturday from seven to nine. Are you in or out?"

He blows out a gusty breath. "Okay. I'm in."

I punch a fist into the air, relief flooding through me. I only need to find one more act. I give him more details about the gig and where he can stay while he's in town and whatnot and then we hang up.

Using a blue marker, I fill in his date on the calendar and step back and look over the work I've done for the past week with satisfaction.

It's been a whirlwind of phone calls and texts, planning and scheduling, while also working and trying to fit in sleeping and eating wherever feasible.

I haven't had a chance to do more than a quick read of the details Georgia emailed me about Mom.

Apparently, there was a woman who lived and worked in Boylesville, Pennsylvania, who had her name legally changed fifteen years ago from Rebecca Fox to Dawn Cooper.

The address Georgia sent me is for an antique store.

The owner might know her. I'll have to stop by during business hours, maybe next week.

Normally, I would be jumping at the chance to follow another trail that might lead to answers. But right now, the thought of following the lead doesn't excite me.

I shove the thought away. I have to get back to work.

I've been swamped, but the work has been gratifying. I've actually been enjoying myself, which isn't something I ever thought possible. Liking work? Who does that?

The only downside is I haven't spent much time alone with Atticus since our hike and the mind-blowing afternoon of orgasms that followed.

I've never had one man so focused on my pleasure, like it's his singular goal in life.

As of yesterday, his family is back in town for his cousin's birthday so we have nowhere to hook up except the back of his truck, where we've managed to spend a few minutes here and there making out like teenagers, which has only succeeded in sharpening the lust to a razor's edge.

The office phone rings, and then it keeps ringing, one call after another for over an hour. Then I deal with an employee calling out, an angry customer, and an unannounced visit from the health inspector. The hours fly by until it's time for me to help with the dinner rush.

I'm at the bar, mixing one of my specialties, a gimlet with elderflower liqueur, when Atticus walks in, the sight of his broad shoulders and purposeful stride triggering a rush of heat that coils and settles between my legs.

Damn he's sexy.

He's with his family. Other than a few brief greetings here and there at town functions, the last time I saw them was over a decade ago. Paul's dark hair is shot through with gray, and the laugh lines around Moira's eyes have deepened, but otherwise, they look almost exactly the same. His cousins, on the other hand, were just kids ten years ago. Now they are unrecognizable as adults, all dolled up in summer dresses.

They take a seat in a corner booth and my feet itch to rush over and get their orders, but I manage to suppress the urge. They are in Gloria's section. She can handle it. There's no reason for me to run over there. We're just friends. Totally casual friends.

And yet something continuously tugs my attention to their booth. Part of it is just drinking Atticus in with my eyes, and part of it is sheer curiosity. I want to know more about his family, and his life, especially after everything we've shared.

Marika and Sylvie lean in toward Moira and Paul, engaged in conversation. Atticus sits on the same side as his cousins, but he's positioned slightly off to the side, his posture upright. He's both connected to the group and yet slightly apart.

I frown, thinking about Christmas and how they all went to Bermuda, and what he said on our hike, how he's always the outsider.

Gloria gives me their order, and I make drinks for

the table, filling the tray with Paul's beer, Moira's old-fashioned, and the girls' sodas. Atticus gets a bourbon, the same brand we had together last winter. I shiver.

I need to find a way to get him alone again. And soon. And for more than ten minutes.

My stomach clenches at the thought. "I'll bring out the drinks, Gloria. You can take your break."

She's been on her feet for three hours. She tosses me a relieved smile. "Thanks, Taylor."

I take a breath before winding a careful way through the crowded tables to where Atticus is sitting with his family.

"Hi." I give them all a bright smile. "Paul, Moira, nice to see you both again." I set their drinks down in front of them. "Happy Birthday, Marika. This round is on the house."

"Oh, my goodness, thank you so much," Marika says.

Moira leans forward to pat my arm. "That's so sweet. It's been a long time. I think the last time I saw you was at the Fourth of July last year."

I smile and nod.

"You're working at Veronica's now?" Paul asks.

I tuck my hair behind my ear. "Only temporarily. I'm helping Veronica while she's with her son in Binghamton. His wife is expecting."

"Taylor is managing the whole place for Veronica," Atticus says, his eyes on mine, warm and proud. "She does everything from payroll and scheduling to accounting and dealing with vendors."

"A renaissance woman." Moira smiles at me. "Sounds busy."

"It is," I murmur. An idea strikes me, a way to spend some time with Atticus. Alone. "It's made for some late nights, for sure." I clear my throat and then speak a little louder. "Sometimes I fall asleep on the couch in the office."

"I've done that while studying," Sylvie chimes in. "Wake up with the worst crick in my neck."

"Luckily the couch turns into a bed." My gaze drifts to Atticus.

His eyes lock with mine, understanding burning in the air between us. The corner of his mouth twitches.

We make idle chitchat for a bit until duty calls, and I leave them to get back to work.

I can't wait for this shift to be over. If it wasn't for the crowded restaurant, I might have mauled him right there in the middle of the bar.

It's sort of terrifying how much I crave him. But not terrifying enough to stop.

CHAPTER
Seventeen

ATTICUS

I'm sitting in public with my family, eating dinner, and trying my damnedest to ignore the fact that I'm half hard from Taylor's not-so-subtle hint as to where we can meet up tonight.

All it took was a few words and a simple glance, and I'm hooked.

My family talks, their conversation flowing around me. Moira tells a story about their trip to the Grand Canyon, and my cousins catch us up on their college life and what they're taking next semester.

I half pay attention, since most of my thoughts are gathering around the woman serving drinks at the bar and laughing with the customers.

It's been three days since I've been inside her and

I've thought of little else since. She's burned herself into my brain like an earworm.

"Are you enjoying working at the camp?" Moira asks, drawing my attention back to the conversation at the table.

"Yeah. It's been great."

Paul takes a sip of his beer. "You don't miss all the traveling? Seeing the world?"

"In some ways." I guess I never shared with them how miserable I was, and how much I wanted to live in Whitby full time.

Moira pats my hand. "As long as you're happy."

"I am."

We eat and talk—well, they do most of the talking—and then we head back to the house around nine.

We play a couple rounds of Clue, but I'm barely paying attention to whether it's Colonel Mustard in the library with a candlestick or Miss Scarlet in the study with the gun.

My eyes stray to the clock every ten minutes until everyone heads to bed for the night.

I shut the door to my room and stare at the bed. The same bed Taylor was splayed out on, naked and needy. Every bit of this room has been marked by her presence. Hell, she's marked me too.

I check the time again. I'm leaving as soon as the house settles and everyone is asleep.

My cousins are still awake, their murmured voices loud enough to penetrate the wall between our rooms.

Sylvie and Marika share the room next to mine, their

childhood bedroom. I've always wondered if they resented me for making them share a room when they had their own before I moved in, but I've never asked.

I pick up an old paperback on my desk to try to distract myself, but after going over the same paragraph seven times, I give up.

An hour later, the house is silent and Veronica's has been closed for fifteen minutes. I sneak out the front door, shutting and locking it quietly behind me before climbing into my truck and aiming it toward Veronica's.

The parking lot is empty, except for a Camp Aria Jeep at the back of the lot.

I park next to it and jog to the front door.

It swings open before I reach for the handle.

She is a little more frazzled than she was a few hours ago. Hair wafts around her face, coming loose from her ponytail, her T-shirt is wrinkled, and there's a stain on the hip of her jeans.

She's perfect.

We move together. In a single breath, her arms are around my waist, her lips on mine. My fingers thread into her hair, angling her head to deepen the kiss.

Yes.

She steps back, pulling me along, and I go willingly, walking inside and kicking the door shut behind me.

Taylor is tangled up in the same rush of need, her hands running down the front of my body and plucking at the button on my jeans. "I want you now," she says against my lips.

I spin us around and push her against the wall next

to the door. She lifts one leg, winding it around my leg. I fumble with her pants, managing between kisses to get them undone, and shoved down far enough to slip my hand between her legs and run my fingers across her slick heat.

"You're so wet." I can't disguise the wonder in my voice. It's impossible, unfathomable, that she could want me as much as I want her, but the knowledge ratchets up the arousal coursing through my body by a thousand.

She kisses down my jaw. "All it takes is one look at you and I'm soaked," she whispers, her voice husky.

The admission tightens every inch of my body until I'm sure I'll crack under the strain.

Frantic, we work together to eliminate clothing, shoving pants and underwear off her body. I lift her up against the wall, pressing between her legs. I push my own jeans down just far enough for my erection to spring free and drive into her.

We both groan at the sensation.

"You feel perfect," she says.

Words hover on the tip of my tongue. *You are perfect. You are everything.*

I hold them back and kiss her instead, showing her how adored she is with every brush of my tongue against hers, every thrust of my body, every stroke of my skin against hers.

I trace a line down her body, using my fingers to apply pressure to the bundle of nerves at the apex of her thighs, increasing my tempo, plunging into her over and over, faster and faster.

She pants, our mouths breaking apart. "Atticus, oh my God, I'm going to come."

"Do it."

As if triggered by my words, she breaks apart, her inner muscles clenching around me. She gasps my name as she shatters, the sound triggering my own release.

Stars explode behind my eyes. Pure bliss floods my entire body. The world disappears and all that's left is the woman in my arms and the synchronicity of our mingled breaths, our pounding hearts.

Her head drops to my shoulder. "That was amazing," she pants. "Exactly what I needed. I've missed this."

My heart soars at her words. It's only been a few days. Maybe she'll miss it enough to stay.

My soaring heart tumbles at the reminder of her departure, and I shove the emotions to the side.

We have right now.

"We're just getting started." My cock is only half deflated, I could go for round two right now, but this time I want to take it a little slower.

Holding her under her thighs, I shift us away from the wall and carry her through the bar and down the hall into the back office.

The door is ajar. I kick it the rest of the way with my foot and take her inside to the couch, kicking my pants off the rest of the way and sitting down so she's perched in my lap, straddling my thighs.

"Too many clothes." I nip at her jaw.

She grabs the bottom of her shirt, pulling it up and over her head.

Her bra is bright pink, her chest heaving directly in my eyeline. I could take in her flawless skin for hours.

She reaches behind her back, unclasping her bra and tossing it behind her. "Now it's my turn."

I swallow hard, my hands clenching around her hips.

She reaches down, lifting my shirt over my head. It joins her bra on the floor. Her hands trace over my chest. "I love your body."

My pulse races at the word *love* emerging from her lips.

For endless minutes, we get lost in each other, in the glide of hands over skin, in the way she rides me, slowly and with single-minded focus, taking control of our pleasure.

When she falls over the edge, the ripple of her inner muscles yanks the release from my body. With a harsh groan, I spend inside her, my arms clenching, holding her tighter and tighter like I'm attempting to meld our bodies together.

I shift us to lay on the couch, rearranging our positions so she's sprawled on top of me. "Did I hurt you?" I can't stop touching her, memorizing skin with my fingertips, luxuriating in the silky strands of hair spread across my chest.

"No." Her lips tip up at the corners. "Not at all."

She blows out a breath, the air gusting over my chest. "We can't wait so long until the next time. If I have to forgo this another week, I might combust."

"I know."

She props her chin on the back of her hand, her fingers brushing my chest as she meets my eyes. "How long is your family in town?"

"Until Monday. Paul and Moira are making a quick trip to Niagara Falls for their anniversary, and they'll be back next week. My cousins are heading back to Boston. They have summer jobs to get back to before the next term starts."

She smiles. "Then I'll be the one sneaking out to see you. You know, it would be easier if you were living in one of the counselor cabins. Although Finley mentioned the housing costs for people who stay on site come out of the stipend, so I guess living rent-free is a plus."

"I pay rent."

She frowns. "What? Why?"

I shrug. "I insist on it. "

Her nose wrinkles. "But they're family. And you're housesitting for them, doing them a favor."

I don't know how to explain it. "I owe them everything. Without them, I would have been shuffled into the foster care system and who knows what would have become of me? I was sent to a temporary, emergency shelter while the state sorted out the next of kin. I was only there a couple of days, and I was lucky for it.

There were kids who were left there for months. Rent is the least I can do."

One hand comes up to cup my cheek. "You think they did you a favor. And you want to repay them." Her eyes search mine. "Atticus, you aren't a burden. You weren't a burden to them when you were a teen, and you aren't now."

I rub a strand of her hair between my fingers, unable to meet her soft gaze. "But I was."

"How could you think that?"

I drop her hair, wrapping my arm around her back. "Six months after I moved in with them, I overheard them talking. They thought I was asleep, but I didn't sleep well for a long time after my parents passed. I was growing a lot, eating a lot, outgrowing pants and shirts faster than they could buy them." I sigh and avert my eyes from hers, staring up at the ceiling. "My parents were young. They didn't have much life insurance, and the survivor's benefits from the government were barely enough to cover my upkeep. Plus Paul and Moira had two other kids. They were stressed, and worried about paying for their college, let alone adding another kid to the mix."

It was one of the reasons I did so well in school, and worked so hard. In part, it was an escape from my past, and it was also the need to not be an inconvenience to anyone. At least, not any more than I already was."

"You were just a child. A child who had lost his parents. None of what happened was your fault."

"But it was my fault. It was all my fault."

Her brows furrow. "What do you mean?"

I've never told anyone what happened before my parents died, but for some reason, staring into Taylor's warm eyes, the urge to confess overwhelms me.

I should be terrified to reveal my truths. It might send her running, but then she's going to do that eventually anyway. And something inside me aches to tell her. She's the only person I could trust with the bruised pieces of my past.

"My parents were separating. They planned on getting a divorce before they died."

Her brows lift in surprise but she remains silent, waiting.

"They told me a week before they died. They weren't in love anymore. It wasn't a dramatic split. Things had just changed between them. But I was so angry and hurt. I didn't understand. I lashed out. I told them I hated them. I was a complete little dick."

Shame burns through me. At the time, the betrayal was all I could focus on. I was selfish. Spoiled. I wish I could go back in time and shake that kid and tell him to appreciate what he had before it was gone.

"You were only a child."

"I was old enough." I shut my eyes. "They went out to dinner to discuss some of the details of the separation without me there, and then they never came home."

Her lips brush against the skin on my chest, gentle, soothing, a benediction.

"It was an accident. Mom was driving. She swerved and hit a tree. They think there might have been a deer or something in the road." A lump builds in my throat and I swallow it down. "The last thing I said to them was 'I don't care.' " I blink my eyes open.

Taylor is watching me with eyes full of sympathy, not pity, not horror or judgment. Her fingers weave into my hair and she presses her lips against mine, a light, tender touch.

Her thumb wipes the wetness off my cheek.

"It was a terrible, senseless accident. It wasn't your fault."

"I know. It doesn't stop the guilt."

She nods, her eyes searching mine. "I get it." There's pain etched in her face, pain that isn't mine, but I recognize it all the same.

My head cocks to one side. "What is it?"

She swallows. "I was one of the last people to see Aria alive. I'm the one who told the twins to go home, that night right before their accident, knowing neither had a driver's license. They snuck out of the house to follow me to some party—one of them must have overheard me talking about it on the phone. I didn't realize they had followed me. I told them to go home, then they did, and she died. It haunted me. It still haunts me."

I brush her hair back from her face. "You're no more to blame than I am."

She bites her lip. "It was my fault. I should have left with them. I should have made sure they got home safely. But I didn't. I didn't want to leave the party. The guilt ate me alive for years. And then I shared the details with Mindy and she completely lost it on me. She blamed me for Aria's death and never let me forget it—for years."

Ah. So this is the source of the fight. "She didn't mean it. She was hurting too. I'm sure she used it as an excuse. When you're hurting, the easiest thing to do is project all those feelings onto someone else."

She frowns. "Why couldn't she be like us and just blame herself?"

I smile. "Most people like to have someone else to lash out at."

She wrinkles her nose. "I know. You're right. She admitted as much to me last year and apologized and all that. But for nearly a decade, she treated me like shit. And now I'm supposed to what, pretend it never happened?"

Her guilt, her pain about the past wraps around my heart and squeezes. It mirrors my own. "No, you shouldn't pretend anything. You're right to feel hurt. To be upset, to be angry, to feel whatever you feel. But I don't think this is about forgiving her. Can you forgive yourself?"

She shakes her head. "I don't know. Can you?"

"I don't know either." I pick up her hand, weaving our fingers together.

Her eyes dip to where our hands are joined. "Maybe we can both try."

"Maybe we can."

She bites her lip. "Although, I'm not sure anyone in

my family will forgive me when I tell them about something I've been keeping secret for a while."

"What is it?"

She squeezes my hand. "The thing is . . . I've been looking for our mom."

CHAPTER
Eighteen

TAYLOR

I hold my breath, waiting for his reaction.

His head dips and he brushes a kiss against my mouth. A silent message that whispers understanding. "Why haven't you told them?"

The tension inside me relaxes. I should have known he would respond with curiosity and not judgment. "They hate her. Rightfully so. She left when we were so young, and none of us really understand why. I was only two. The twins were barely one. We never knew her, and I guess I want to know what she was like. Finley and Mindy are the only ones who remember anything about her, and they don't talk about it."

His free hand trails up my arm. "What made you want to look for her after all this time?"

"We were going through Dad's room and I found a

picture of her and it was," I shrug, "I don't know, it was weird. I had never seen her before and I had never thought about her much. She was always some distant, unimportant figure from my past who didn't matter. But then seeing her face, it was like suddenly she became a real person with hopes and dreams and demons. I guess . . . I want to know if I'm like her."

His brows dip. "What do you mean, like her?"

My fingers twitch, still in his grasp. "Never able to stay in one place. The type of person who can leave everyone behind."

The itch under my skin, the thrumming in my veins to go and go and never stop . . . is that why Mom left, because she felt the urge to run like I do?

I want to hate her. But am I no better than she is? Is being a deadbeat genetic?

He lifts my hand and kisses the back of it. "You love your family, Taylor. You don't leave them behind, even when you're not here."

I suppose that's true. I could never cut them out of my life completely, it would be like severing a limb.

"Your dad never mentioned anything about why your mom might have left?"

"I vaguely remember something about her being depressed, but I don't know if I heard that from Dad or Finley. She had six kids in eight years. It's a lot for anyone, I guess. But to leave us all there, to leave Dad alone? How could she? Dad was great, but we needed *her*."

I needed her. But more than anything, Finley needed

her. Finley never really had a childhood, since she became a surrogate mother. I'm angry. Confused. I need to know *why*. I need to make sense of it.

"You think they would be upset with you if they knew you've been trying to find her?"

A frown tugs at my lips. "I don't know. Maybe."

It's not so much that I think they would be angry with me. I'm not sure if they would understand. They don't have this same urge, the same need to run, to avoid. Like me, like Mom. This search has been personal. Something I need to do on my own, without having to defend the actions to anyone. Besides, they would probably insist on helping or getting involved in some way. They have enough going on in their lives right now. The last thing I want to do is add to their stress, their worries. What if I don't find anything? What if it's all for nothing?

I shake the thoughts away and tell Atticus everything. How I hired a PI. How I've been searching the country since last year, following leads. "I'm going to go to this antique store next week in Pennsylvania. It was the last known mailing address of someone named Dawn Cooper, who legally changed her name from Rebecca Fox. The owner of the store, his name is Jonas something or other. Maybe he knows her, or where I can find her."

His eyes get stormy. "You're going to go meet some strange man hours away and you weren't going to tell anyone?"

I grin at his scowl. "You're so cute when you're

worried. I'm telling you now. Besides it's a store. Public."

His hand tightens on my hip. "Still."

"My PI vetted him, he's not a serial killer." I shrug. "Probably."

A discontented hum rumbles in his chest.

Laughter bubbles out of me. "You want to come with me or are you growly because you want to show me your angry raccoon impression?"

He huffs out a laugh. "I am going with you."

"Good. I didn't want to go alone anyway. You don't have to work next week?"

"We could go on Monday. Campers won't be here until Wednesday, so it shouldn't be an issue." His hand rubs down my back in a soothing gesture.

Everything inside me goes to mush at his easy acquiescence, at the simple affection. It's been so long since I've been able to share pieces of myself with someone else without fear. Ever since Mindy lashed out at me after Aria's death, opening up to anyone has been a struggle. But not with Atticus.

In a month, this will be over.

Dread sinks through me but I push it down further, somewhere deep where it can't reach up and hurt me.

I lift up to press my lips against his, banishing everything else to the wind.

Reaching down, I wrap my fingers around his cock and he immediately hardens under my touch.

A desperate sort of madness sucks us both into its grip. Atticus groans, taking my face in his warm palms and kissing me hard, the contrast between his gentle hands and fervent lips intoxicating. Ecstasy swirls and beckons, and I plunge into it headfirst, ignoring the inevitable future battering at my heart.

We may not have a future, but we have right now and I intend to make the most of it.

Knocking rouses me from slumber.

"Go away," I mumble into the pillow.

The knocking comes again, accompanied by the creak of the bedroom door and Finley's voice. "Taylor? Are you awake?"

I groan.

"Can I talk to you for a second?"

Without opening my eyes, I grab the extra pillow next to my head and chuck it in her general direction. I spent the early morning hours with Atticus and I swear my head just hit the pillow ten minutes ago.

She laughs. "Now that you're awake, can we talk for a second?"

"No," I whine, lifting the blankets up to cover my head.

Clearly undaunted by my verbal discontent or projectile bedding, the mattress dips as she settles near my waist.

I flip the blankets down and blink at her. "Seriously? What time is it?"

"Almost noon. Don't you have to go to Veronica's soon? What time did you get home anyway?"

I scrub at my face. "Late." I pause and then make an attempt to avoid further questioning. "I had some paperwork and things to do." Which is true, if Atticus can be considered "things," and I did spend all night on him.

The fog of sleep is drifting away, clarity returning. My gaze sharpens on Finley's face and the way her lips purse in thought, the groove between her brows, and the way she's fidgeting with the hem of her T-shirt.

"What's up, Fin?"

"I wanted to ask you something before you left. I have to greet the new counselors that are coming in for the camp that starts next week," she glances at her watch, "soon."

I shift onto my side to face her more fully. "Ask away."

"I was talking to Mindy and—"

I groan. "Finley."

She holds up a palm. "Just hear me out. Please. I swear I'm not going to talk about you two reconciling or anything. This is something else."

Ugh. "Fine."

"She signed this amazing band with one of the most talented singer-songwriters she's ever met, an almost complete unknown who would be perfect for one of the performances you're setting up at Veronica's." She watches me, waiting.

I do need one more act to fill the last Saturday night

available. And no matter my personal animosity toward Mindy, there is no denying she has excellent taste in music. She signed some of the biggest bands in the country when she was working at Rebel Records. I would be foolish not to at least give this band a chance. "I'm listening. What's the band like?"

She grins. "They're sort of pop funk, I guess. They call themselves Discontinued Barbies."

A laugh huffs out of me. Good name.

Finley smiles, encouraged by my response. "She has some other industry peeps she can invite too who might be interested in the other talent you've got going. We had this idea where you could pool your resources."

Great. They've been talking about me. Again. But the thought doesn't make me as angry as it once did. They're not talking shit, after all.

"So in exchange for letting this band have a spot, she'll bring in more interest." I blow out a breath. It's a good idea. Great idea, even. But . . . "I don't want to talk to Mindy."

"You don't have to talk. You can text or email. She won't even come to the performance if you don't want her here. She said she can send the band on their own or with their manager and you can schedule it through them."

I sigh. I don't want to live up to what Mindy always used to accuse me of, being the immature little sister who can't get her act together and behaves like a brat instead of an adult. I'm twenty-seven years old. I can be mature. Sometimes.

"I'll reach out to Mindy today and listen to Discontinued Barbies and see if they'll be a good fit."

Finley beams, reaching over to pat my leg, her touch muffled by the comforter. "I'll let you rest before you have to get up and get ready."

She practically slips out the door, shutting it behind her.

I fluff my pillow and roll onto my stomach, shutting my eyes.

Sleep, I direct my brain. It doesn't take much prodding. I'm halfway to dreamland when the door shoves open, hitting the wall.

"Hey." Jake plops down on the bed, sitting exactly where Finley was minutes ago. "Can I talk to you?"

I groan. "Don't you knock?"

"Why would I do that?"

I roll my eyes. "I don't know, common decency?"

"Huh." He scratches his head. "Anyway, I wanted to talk to you before I left because I did what you recommended."

"What? You finally figured out how to pee *in* the toilet instead of on every surface around it?"

"Uh, do we really want to trade barbs on bathroom habits? Don't get me started with your hair on the shower wall. Why do you do that? Are you suffering from premature balding?" He tugs on a strand of my hair.

I swipe his hand away. "I'm trying to keep my hair from clogging the drain, you're welcome. I just forget to throw it in the trash sometimes."

His mouth spreads into a grimace. "It's hard to imagine why you're still single."

I grab my pillow and whack him with it.

He plucks it out of my hands and tosses it across the room.

"Jake!"

"You started it."

Ugh. Brothers. "Anyway." I reach for the other pillow and tuck it under my head. "What did you want to tell me?"

"I hired someone to help me look for the letter writer." His nose scrunches. "It was not as cool as I thought it would be. He wasn't wearing a trench coat and hat with those Groucho glasses. He was some normal middle-aged dude who drove a Mazda. He's looking into things and I just wanted to say thanks for the advice."

"That's great, Jake. Let me know if he finds anything."

"I'll keep you updated."

I reach over to tap on his knee with a fingertip. "Are you going to tell the others?"

He shakes his head. "No. Not yet."

"Why?"

"I don't have any real information at this point. And," he rubs the back of his neck, "this is like *my* thing. It gives me something outside of this place to focus on, you know? It's something I need to do alone. If I tell anyone other than you, everyone else will find out and Finley and Archer already act like I need a nanny."

I chuckle. "I get it." I have my own secret journey, after all.

But I also understand where the perhaps overzealous concern is coming from. Out of all of us, Jake was hit the hardest after Aria's death.

They were twins. Inseparable. Even worse, he was with her when she died. I can't even fathom what he's gone through. He never speaks about it.

Not long after she died, our dad got sick. Jake was his main caretaker, which helped distract him, but after Dad died, Jake escaped his demons by diving into any bottle he could find. None of us, except Finley, realized how bad things had gotten until he crashed the truck over a year ago and ended up in the hospital. He's been mostly sober since, besides a little hiccup last fall.

I wasn't home enough to notice how bad he had gotten. I was too wrapped up in my own life, my own guilt, my own desire to escape my past.

So I understand why Finley and Archer would be worried for him. Why they might want to coddle and cosset him. And I also understand why he needs a goal, a distraction that belongs to him and no one else.

"No one has asked you about the letters since last year?"

He wrinkles his nose. "Finley did once, in passing, but she didn't seem to care much. Our sisters are too distracted with everything else going on around here.

"If you need anything, you know I'm always here, right? Even if I'm not actually here."

He reaches over and scrubs my hair with his knuckles. "Duh."

I smack his hand away and then roll over. "Now go away, I'm tired."

He chuckles and leaves the room, but it's a while before I can fall asleep.

CHAPTER
Nineteen

"Are you okay?" Atticus reaches over the center console, his broad hand covering mine where my fist is clenched in my lap.

I pull my gaze from where I've been staring sightlessly out the window and look over at him. "Yes. No. I don't know."

He frowns. "Do you want to talk about it?"

I flip my hand in his, linking our fingers. "No. Distract me."

The corner of his mouth quirks up and he shoots me a heated glance. "The distraction I have in mind is rather tone-deaf, considering what we're doing today."

This is the first time in his presence my mind isn't flooded with thoughts of sex and my body isn't heated. He's right, while I would love to have some truly fun car times, all I can think about is meeting this Jonas person and if he knows where Mom is. What if she lives in this town? What if she doesn't? Will I meet her? What if she's dead? What if she doesn't want to be found?

"Tell me about plants." I lean my head back against the headrest and stare at his profile.

He tosses me a quick grin, and my heart leaps. He's so handsome. I could stare at his profile all day, taking in the stubble outlining his strong jaw, the flex of his arms as he navigates the car. Even the grip of his fingers on the wheel is hot.

He clicks on the blinker and glances into his blind spot before changing lanes. "You really want me to tell you things about plants? That will distract you?"

Just sitting next to him, and the deep rumble of his voice, is soothing. "Absolutely."

"Fine. You asked for it. But if you fall asleep it's on you."

We drive in silence for a few seconds before he speaks. "Did you know that plants talk with each other?"

My brows lift. "What? How?"

"Through their roots. They secrete chemicals called root exudates. There are studies that suggest plants can tell if another plant is their sibling—if they're grown from seeds from the same parent plant."

My mouth pops open. "No way."

He glances over at me. "Yep. When they are placed near a strange plant, their root allocation increases— they spread their roots more to fight for access to water and soil nutrients. But when they're near siblings, they are more accommodating of each other."

I wrinkle my nose. "Really? Huh. If someone put me in a pot with Jake, it would be like *The Hunger Games*."

He chuckles.

Our conversation flows as we drive on, and oddly enough, talking about plants is a good distraction. Or maybe it's just Atticus.

Before I know it, he's coming to a stop outside of a two-story residence. It's a Victorian-style home with red siding and white shutters. Flower boxes adorn the windows, spilling over with an effusion of white and blue flowers. I wouldn't know it was a store if it weren't for the sign next to the front door that reads *Boylesville Antiques* in an old-style font.

Atticus eyeballs it and then me, searching my face. "Are you ready?"

My palms prickle with sweat. "I'm not sure."

His hand covers mine. "Take your time. We can come back another day. Whatever you need." He turns back to the window, giving me a moment, keeping the car on and the AC running.

My heart jolts in my chest. How can I leave him behind? Just thinking of our inevitable end has the power to rip me in two. How am I ever going to return, knowing he's no longer mine to touch, to taste, to have the right to simply *be* with, as we are now?

I can't dwell on any of this right now. I focus on breathing and on the task ahead.

After a few minutes, I open the passenger door.

He turns off the car and we step out into the midday summer heat.

The porch boards creak under our feet as we approach the front door.

We stand on the stoop while I stare at the *Open* sign suction-cupped to the window and try to calm the anxiety swirling through my gut.

Atticus pushes the door open, holding it for me to precede him inside.

A bell jingles overhead.

We step into a room that could have been a living room at one time, but it's been converted into a sales floor. It's cluttered but clean. Shelves line the back wall, stuffed with small tchotchkes and books and vases. An old magazine stand rests in one corner, full of old *National Geographic*s and *Post Magazine*s. Furniture is scattered around the space, dotted with bright white placards announcing the price for each item. In the front, a couple of clothes racks are crowded with plastic-encased suits, dresses, and jackets.

"I'll be out in a minute," a masculine voice calls from somewhere deeper inside the house.

I can barely focus on the items around me, my hands shaky with nerves, while emotions battle in my chest: anticipation threaded with anxiety and shaken up with trepidation.

Finally, a man emerges through a back door, striding over to greet us. He's middle-aged with a full head of gray hair, and thick-framed glasses perched on the bridge of his nose. "Welcome in. Is there anything I can help you find?"

"Hi, yeah. Are you Jonas Mesa?" I reach into my bag, pulling out the photo of Mom and gripping it in my fingers.

"Yes, I am."

"We're looking for someone you might know." I hand him the picture.

He takes the photo, holds it closer to his face, and inspects it. "She looks younger, but this looks like Dawn Cooper."

My heart thuds in my chest, reverberating through my ears so loud I'm sure it's echoing in the room. "You know her?"

His eyes flick to Atticus, gaze guarded. "Who's asking?"

"She's my mother."

His eyes widen. "Are you Finley?"

My stomach drops to my toes. "No. I'm Taylor, Finley is my sister. How did you—" I break off, not sure how to even continue the question.

"Dawn would talk about her sometimes, toward the end."

A lump lodges in my throat, my mind racing.

It's her, it's her, it's her, combined with the echo of his words over and over. I speak them out loud, needing to know, unable to connect the dots through the roaring in my ears. "The end?"

"She passed away two years ago."

The knowledge sinks into my skin, the information overload leaving me emotionally whiplashed.

He knew her.

She's gone. I'm too late. Why did I wait? Why did I bother searching in the first place, only to end up here?

What now?

Atticus slides his hand into mine, his fingers gripping with a comforting pressure.

"Will you tell me about her?" I ask.

He nods. "Yeah. Maybe you can answer some of my questions too."

"Of course." What little I know I have no reason not to share.

"Then come on to the back, we can chat more comfortably in here." He jerks a thumb behind him.

Five minutes later, Atticus and I are sitting on a worn leather sofa in an office in the back of the house. I'm clutching a glass of water, but I haven't been able to take a sip.

"How did you know her?" I ask.

Jonas sits at his desk, in a high-back swivel chair, facing us. "My mother, Carla, was friends with Dawn for many years. Mom was a nurse in Scranton. They met at the hospital. Dawn was initially brought in as a Jane Doe."

Shock pins me to my seat. "What happened?"

"She was found in a hotel room, unconscious. She had tried to kill herself."

I gasp, my hand covering my mouth. "I had no idea."

"She struggled a lot with depression. But she did better after she got on meds. Mom took her in and helped her get a job in town at the diner."

"That was very kind of your mother."

He rests his elbows on the desk, steepling his fingers in front of him. "They were close. When Mom got sick with Parkinson's, Dawn moved into the guest house out back and helped me with her care." He gestures behind him. "Then when Dawn got sick three years ago, I took care of her. She was like a second mother, in some ways."

Like a second mother. The words echo through me. A second mother to someone who wasn't her child. Why couldn't she be our first mother?

I swallow and force the next words out. "How did she die?"

"Pneumonia. Her immune system was weak, from the dementia."

Unthinking, I reach for Atticus, his fingers effortlessly entwining with my own.

"Did she ever say anything about her past?"

"Not until the end, when her mind was gone. She would call out for Finley sometimes, and say things like she was talking to someone."

I take a small sip of my water and then set it on a coaster on a side table. "What did she say?"

He scratches the back of his head. "I couldn't really track it. She would talk about random things, like she was finishing a conversation that had started twenty years ago."

"She never mentioned anyone other than Finley?"

"I'm sorry. No."

My mind is spinning.

Nothing about the rest of us, the twins, Mindy, Piper, or me? Why? I'll never know. It's too late. The thought is unsettling, leaving me off balance.

I'm still processing the information overload when Jonas speaks. "She would never talk about her past before she came here. Can you tell me what you know? Where she came from?"

Numbly, I nod. "She's from Whitby, in New York. She . . . I don't know why she left us."

His brows lift. "Us?"

"Me and my siblings. There were six of us."

He rocks back in his seat, face blanching with shock. "Six children? I didn't know." He scrubs a hand through his hair. "I had no idea Dawn left so many behind."

I don't know what to say, or how to respond. I'm not even sure what to think.

Jonas's eyes are wide. "I can't believe she never said anything to us. She never gave us details about her life except to say she was from New York and that she left a difficult relationship. We assumed it was abusive or something."

"It wasn't. My dad was great. Never lifted a hand in anger." The man couldn't even kill spiders and insisted on capture and release. "Finley is my oldest sister. She was eight when Mom left, Mindy was seven, Piper was four, I was two, and she had twin babies. Jake and Aria were only one."

As I speak, listing all my siblings, his eyes grow wider and wider. "Aria? That's someone's name?"

I squeeze Atticus's hand harder. "Yes. Why?"

"Before she passed, she said Aria, multiple times. I didn't realize it was a person's name. She would say something about beautiful Aria, and her eyes would focus on something beyond me, like she was speaking to someone else. I thought it was gibberish. I assumed she was referring to some kind of song. She loved music, especially opera."

Chills spread up my arms at the details. She loved music. Like me. Like Mindy. I guess we come by the obsession honestly. "Aria is dead."

He presses his lips together, his head dipping forward. "I'm so sorry. How long has she been gone?"

"Eleven years."

He rubs his chin. "A week before she passed, Dawn made one of her Aria comments. She told me Aria had been there to visit and was coming back for her. I couldn't track what she meant at the time—I didn't even consider Aria was someone's name. So much of what she talked about was nonsensical."

My eyes burned, growing warm with unshed tears.

Jonas clears his throat, shuffling behind the desk to stand. "Did you want to see where she lived? I kept a box of her things, the personal items she left behind, just in case. There isn't much. But it's out there at the house."

"Yes, please."

We follow Jonas out the front door and around the side of the house to the back, down a dirt road to a smaller structure.

The front door opens into a narrow living space, dusty from disuse and half full of boxes, along with an old, torn, and sagging couch.

"No one's lived here since Dawn passed. I didn't rent it out. Decided to use it for storage and overflow from the shop," Jonas explains, moving into the kitchenette and rearranging some boxes on the counter.

I take a quick glance around. There are only two doors off the living space, maybe leading to a bedroom and bathroom.

"Here." Jonas hands me a medium-sized box, along with a shoebox.

They're light, no more than fifteen pounds.

"I've got to head back out to the store, so I'll give you some time and space to look through these now if you like. Feel free to take that with you when you leave," he gestures to the boxes, "share with your siblings." He still looks a bit shell-shocked about the afternoon's revelations, shaking his head slowly before saying, "I can't believe Dawn left so many children behind." He blows out a breath. "If you have any questions before you leave, I'll be in the house. And if you choose to take off, I understand. Here's my card if you need to talk about anything or have any other questions I can answer later."

"Thank you."

Jonas nods in acknowledgment and leaves.

I stare down at the boxes in my hand, unsure what to do.

Atticus takes both from me, setting them on a scratched wooden side table. "Do you want me to stay?"

I meet his gaze. "Yes. Please."

Picking up the shoebox, we perch side by side on the dusty couch and I take a deep breath before popping open the lid.

At the top of the box are old pay stubs.

I blink. "That's not what I expected."

"What did you expect?"

I shrug. "I don't know, a cryptic letter with clues to follow that leads us on a week-long scavenger hunt across the country and ends in us stealing the Declaration of Independence?"

He nudges me with his shoulder, chuckling. "Funny."

I flip through the pay stubs before setting them to the side. "I guess I want answers. Something to explain why she left, something to show she actually gave a crap."

Underneath are some loose photos. One of Mom with an older woman, standing on a bridge overlooking a narrow river. Above them stretches a blue sky studded with fluffy white clouds. They're smiling, standing next to each other. It must be Carla, Jonas's mom. There are more photos, some with Mom, and some without. One is a group photo of strangers.

They're standing outside of a restaurant. Maybe the diner she worked at.

I hand the photos to Atticus and then reach in and pull out a necklace. It's a short silver chain, rusty with age, a phoenix dangling from the end. The wings of the bird are spread wide, with multiple layers to the setting, adding dimension to the pendant.

It's the same necklace she wore in the photo I found in Dad's room. I've stared at it so many times over the past six months, it's almost unreal that I'm holding it in my hands.

I drop it back in the box, my chest tight. "I can't." My voice is scratchy and thick. Something about this isn't right. It's too much. Overwhelming.

I should be doing this with my family.

The realization washes over me, erasing the sense of wrongness that had taken over seconds before.

"I need to do this with my siblings."

Atticus lifts his arm and I snuggle into his side, immediately easing when his scent surrounds me, and he wraps me up against him. "It's okay."

He doesn't say anything else. He doesn't have to. He sits there with me while I try and process everything and breathe.

Minutes pass in silence.

How would I have done this without him? I guess it would have been okay, but I can't imagine how I would be dealing with the overwhelming panic erupting through me if I didn't have his support, his quiet strength.

I stare down at the picture of Mom on the top of the pile. *Why? Why did you leave? Why didn't you come back when you got better? Why did you try to kill yourself?*

I don't know if we'll ever have answers. It's like a loose thread, a frustrating one that hangs down and tickles a place you can't scratch.

Part of this search has been an excuse to run away, from my past, from my own bad decisions, from guilt and the worry and the shame and the pain.

What do I do now?

CHAPTER

Twenty

Atticus

We stop at a little diner twenty minutes outside of Boylestown, not the same as the one in the photo in Mom's box. It's one of those places with black-and-white checkboard floors, red vinyl booths, and a miniature jukebox at every table.

Sitting in a booth near the back, we soak in the scent of greasy food that permeates the room, probably leaking out of the walls themselves at this point, and look over the plastic-covered menus.

Taylor rubs her stomach. "Everything sounds good right now. I don't know why, but having an emotional meltdown sure does stir up an appetite."

I chuckle. "You have fairly tame meltdowns." She has been quiet since we left the antique store, only speaking when asked a direct question, lost in her own thoughts.

The server stops at our table, a sixty-something woman with dyed red hair wearing a blue dress and a white apron. We both order cheeseburgers and milkshakes.

After she leaves to put in our orders, Taylor reaches over, flicking through the song list on the mini jukebox. "I guess I don't know how to process what I'm feeling. I'm frustrated that I won't ever understand why she left. I can't ask her. I can't demand answers."

"Is that what you would do if she was still alive?"

She rubs her lips together. "I don't know. It doesn't matter because the opportunity is gone. She was so close, all this time. I never thought she would only be a few hours away. She stayed here for decades. Why couldn't she stay with us?" She leans back in the booth, crossing her arms over her chest. "It makes me angry. She left Dad with six kids." She shakes her head. "Did she care? Did she know about Piper's success or Aria's death? We'll never know. How could she do it? What kind of mother does that?"

"A troubled one."

She nods. "Right? And knowing that makes me feel guilty because clearly she was struggling if she ran away and tried to kill herself. If she was dealing with a mental health condition, it wasn't her fault. She probably thought we were better off without her, but even knowing all that, I'm still mad."

I reach out and cover her hand. "It's okay to not be okay. It's okay to be angry and confused and upset."

The corners of her mouth tilt the smallest bit upward. "Thank you. And thank you for being there with me today. I couldn't have done it without you."

"Sure you could have. I was just your emotional support animal."

She gives another closed-mouth smile. "You were great. Now I don't know how I'm going to tell my family the truth."

"You have some time to find the words."

She blows out a breath. "I know. I don't want to wait too long though. I'm sick of having secrets. I'm sick of feeling angry and upset and guilty every time I come home."

"Because of Mindy."

"Yeah. At least in part. I wonder . . . I wonder if part of the reason I can't let go of my anger at Mindy is because it's easier to focus on that, rather than the real reason behind our fight."

I rest my elbows on the table. "That makes sense. Forgiveness is hard. It's easier to forgive strangers than the people we care about. The betrayal cuts deeper when it's someone you love."

She frowns. "Shit. I may have to accept that I actually love that asshole sister of mine, which means I have to forgive her, don't I?"

"You don't have to do anything."

She releases a sigh, settling back in her seat.

The waitress arrives with our food and we eat in comfortable silence.

Halfway through the meal, my phone dings with a text. I glance at the message. "Sorry." I silence the notification.

She waves a hand. "No worries."

I slip the phone back into my pocket. "It's just Aunt Moira, asking if I'll be home for dinner tonight."

"How are things going with your family?" She dips a fry in her milkshake.

"It's been fine." I take a big bite of my burger.

Her brows lift. "Fine? That good, huh?"

"I don't really know how to make things better between us," I admit.

"Have you thought about, I don't know, talking to them?"

Humor twists my lips. "I'm not sure what to say. They aren't doing anything wrong. I don't want them to feel like I'm being critical."

She taps her finger on the table. "But you're not happy."

I shrug. "I just want us to be closer."

She picks up a fry and points it at me. "There. That's it. Tell them exactly that. Ask them to hang out together more. That kind of thing."

Nerves coil in my stomach. "Do you think it's that simple?"

What if they don't want to spend time with me? What if they say no? I don't know how to ask for what I need. I'm the one who's shut myself off from them in my attempt to be accommodating and not a heavy weight around their necks. How do I tell them the truth? It's been too long. Am I too late?

One of her shoulders lifts in a semblance of a shrug. "You never know until you try."

I lean toward her. "I'll make you a deal. You talk to your family, and I'll talk to mine."

She smiles, the first real one she's given me all day. "Deal."

By the time I'm sitting down to dinner later that night, my stomach is twisted in knots.

I half listen as Paul and Moira chat about an upcoming trip to visit a friend in Stony Point, only an hour or so away.

I still don't know how to broach the topic of spending more time with my family, but almost immediately, an opportunity presents itself.

"We can go golfing at Patriot Hills, I've heard it's a great course. Atticus, you want some bread to dip in your soup?" Moira passes me the bread bowl.

Paul finishes chewing. "Yeah. Patriot Hills would be great."

I take the bread bowl and set it next to my bowl of soup. "I could go too."

Their gazes swing toward me at the same time. Paul's spoon is lifted halfway to his mouth and Moira's eyebrows are nearly touching her hairline.

My face heats. "I mean, if you want. It's not far. Just let me know when you're going, and I could meet you there."

Paul finds his voice first. "You like golf?"

"I've never tried it. But I'd like to."

Moira wipes her mouth with her napkin, swallowing her food and glancing over at Uncle Paul before answering. "That would be great. We would love that."

But I can't tell if she means it. She sounds . . . confused.

"Are you sure?"

"Of course. Do you have clubs?"

I hesitate. "No." I put my spoon down, wiping my sweating palms on my knees. "It's not just about golf. It's about spending time with my family." The only family I have left.

Silence stretches out between us, except for the tick of the old cuckoo clock on the wall and my heart thudding in my ears.

Moira hiccups and then covers her mouth. "I'm sorry," she says, her voice thick. "I didn't think you wanted to."

It takes me almost a minute to register her words. "You . . . didn't?"

Moira shakes her head. "You always wanted to keep yourself apart and put up these walls between you and the world. We noticed it when you first came here, and you were so quiet and polite. You were the perfect child, but you had gone through such a terrible loss."

I frown. "And that was a problem?"

Paul shakes his head. "Not a problem. But you were just a kid who'd lost his parents. The girls would get in trouble every other week."

"You wanted me to get in trouble?"

She reaches across the table, putting her hand over mine. "We wanted you to be free to make mistakes. To be happy. We knew you were hurting, and we thought the walls would come down eventually and you needed space and time to know you were safe. But then as the months went on, we didn't know what to do. We didn't know how to get through to you, to get you to talk or open up."

They exchange a glance and then Paul speaks. "We thought you were holding yourself apart because you were frightened to be close to anyone again."

Moira nods. "We worried all the time, wondering if we were doing the right thing by waiting to see if you could feel your way through, find the path forward without us pushing or making you uncomfortable in any way."

I blink in surprise. "I thought I was a burden."

"No," Paul's response is immediate. "Never a burden."

"I heard you talking about how expensive things were."

"Shit," Paul murmurs.

I almost laugh. I've never heard him curse.

Moira leans back removing her hand from over mine to fiddle with her napkin. "Expenses may have been tight here and there, but that was never your fault.

We didn't blame you for our circumstances. That was never on you, you hear me?"

I nod, bewildered.

Paul leans toward Moira. "Should we tell him about the rent money?" he murmurs.

"What do you mean?"

Moira ducks her head. "The money you insisted on giving us for rent, we've been saving for you."

"What?" Shock knocks me back in my seat.

Paul points at me. "We told you we didn't need that money."

They did, but I didn't listen. I wanted to give more than I took because I didn't know how else to repay them.

Moira leans forward, her eyes earnest. "You're doing us a favor, watching the house for us while we travel, that's payment enough."

Paul gives a decisive nod. "Besides, we're family."

"The only reason we took your money was because you were so insistent, and we just want you to be happy." Moira worries her bottom lip, watching my reaction.

I have been more worried about their happiness than my own. I thought if I did enough, if I made the weight of my presence light enough, they wouldn't . . . what, die and leave me with the same feelings of guilt I had after my parents passed?

Meanwhile, they've been trying to respect my boundaries and it's all resulted in this chasm of misunderstanding.

"I'm sorry."

Moira shakes her head. "You have nothing to be sorry for. You just have to be yourself. You're a good person, you don't have to sell yourself to us. Jillian and Patrick would be so proud of the man you've become."

My throat tightens. "Thank you." The words are thick.

Moira stands up and rounds the table, leaning over to hug me.

I pat her on the back.

She clutches me a little tighter. "We'll work on it together. You can always tell us how you feel."

Paul lumbers to his feet too, wrapping an arm around each of us. "You can talk to us about your parents too. Only if you want. And you can go golfing with us, but you have to let me help you pick out your clubs." His eyes gleam.

Moira laughs, the sound choked with emotion. "Shopping for golf supplies has become his favorite pastime. You might regret what you've started."

I swallow past the lump building in my throat, blinking through the stinging in my eyes. "I don't think I will."

CHAPTER
Twenty-One

TAYLOR

Getting all my siblings together in one place, without telling them exactly why we need to be together, is trickier than lassoing a wet noodle with dental floss.

"So, you want me to come to Whitby this weekend to watch some show at Veronica's?" Piper's voice is a mixture of confusion and distraction.

I rub a finger over the spot in my childhood desk where Jake carved his name when he was seven. He used the *A* to also etch in Aria, her name running perpendicular to his.

I need to go into Veronica's soon to get some work done, but first I wanted to set the ball in motion to get my family all together so I can come clean about Mom.

"It's not just any music people, it's Discontinued Barbies. They are one of Mindy's new clients."

There is a weighted pause. "Does that mean you and Mindy are good then? You made up?"

"We haven't. But I'm working on it and this is part of that." Sort of. Maybe.

"And you're asking me to come home because you are trying to help Mindy? That doesn't really make sense. Why wouldn't she ask me herself? We aren't the ones fighting."

"Can't I just want to get all my siblings together for some family bonding time? We haven't been in the same room together since Thanksgiving."

"That's your fault for flaking on Christmas." Her tone is light and teasing, but I know Piper well enough to read the undercurrents.

I tip my head back, shutting my eyes. She's right. I totally flaked. "Piper, I'm sorry about that. Truly I am."

It ended up being a dead end anyway. I went all the way across the country and Mom hadn't left the East Coast.

"You apologized to Finley, right? She was super bummed too, Tay."

"I did and we're good. I promise. Let me make it up to you. Just come to Whitby for a couple of days. Please?"

"Maybe. We'll see. I've been working on more pieces for the gallery and I wanted to have at least one done by the end of the month, but I've gotten nowhere." She blows out a breath, the sound gusting over the phone line. "I haven't felt inspired lately."

I pick up a pen, tapping it against the pad of paper in front of me. "Why? Is everything okay?"

"Everything's fine. I'm in a slump, I guess. It happens."

I frown. "But last time you had creative difficulties it happened because of dickface Ben." Ben, her ex-boyfriend, is now doing hard time for stalking, attempted murder, and defamation, to name just a few of the fucked-up things he did after Piper dumped his abusive ass.

"Well, this time I don't have a psycho ex to blame."

I perk up. "Can we blame Oliver?"

She sighs, but it's a happy sound. "No. He's perfect."

I snort. "He's an ass."

"Yeah, but he's my ass."

A masculine voice echoes in the background and Piper laughs.

"What is he saying?" I ask.

"He wants to know why I'm talking about his ass. You do have a nice ass," she calls out. "Sorry, Taylor, I gotta run. We have a charity event tonight."

"Think about coming this weekend."

"I'll let you know. Love you."

"Love you too, P." I hang up the phone and drop it on the desk.

Even though you're freaking killin' me here.

"Hey." Jake pushes the door open. "You got a second?"

I pick up the pen and throw it at him. "It's called knocking, doofus."

He plops down on the end of the bed, facing me. "What are you doing?"

"I was just talking to Piper. Why? What do you want?"

"Why do you sound so suspicious? Can't I ask random questions and hang out with my favorite older sister?"

"Okay, now I know you want something. Out with it."

He sighs. "I don't want you to get mad at me."

Which means I'm definitely going to get mad.

A tap on the door has both our heads swinging in that direction.

Mindy leans in the doorframe, wearing skinny jeans with heels and a baggy silk blouse. She's holding a manila file in one hand.

Jake bounces off the bed. "I'm getting out of the crossfire. Sorry, Tay, I only did this because she blackmailed me."

Mindy rolls her eyes. "I didn't blackmail you, I asked where Taylor was."

"You bribed me." He points at her. "She brought me pie from Bubby's."

"You asked for that pie three days ago. It had nothing to do with Taylor."

Jake disappears out the door, calling out behind him, "You two can fight. I've got pie waiting for me."

Mindy faces me. "I'll leave if you want, Taylor. I'm

not trying to intrude or bother you. I just wanted to finalize some of the details for the gig, and since I'm here, I thought it would be weird to text from, you know, downstairs." She shifts on her feet.

This is good timing. I need to talk to Mindy anyway, I need to tell her, somehow, that I'm ready to . . . I don't know, try to forgive her? Can I do this? Am I ready? It's only possible if I can trust her with my guilty truths. This whole fight started because I was vulnerable, and she crapped all over me.

There is only one way to know for sure if she means it. If I can trust her again.

I force a smile. "It's fine."

She perches on the edge of the bed, only about a foot away from my chair. Her back is as straight as an arrow, her spine rigid with tension. "So I have the signed performance contract here and we had a question about—"

"I've been looking for Mom," I blurt out.

She stares at me, her face frozen in stunned shock. "What?"

Moment of truth. Will she freak out and lose her mind like she did when I told her about Aria?

"You know, that lady who birthed us and disappeared? I hired a PI and I've spent the last seven months trying to track her down. And I just found out what happened to her."

Her mouth pops open. She shuts it with an audible click and swallows before asking, "What did you find?"

I search her eyes. She's not angry. She's surprised and curious. "She's dead."

She blows out a breath, leaning forward and propping her elbows on her knees, her hands covering her face. "Jesus."

"I'm sorry, I know it's a lot. It's just . . . I haven't told anyone."

Then I give her the whole story. How I hired Georgia, how I've been following leads all over the country trying to find her, and how I finally tracked her down to Boylesville and the subsequent conversation with Jonas. I leave out Atticus but explain how I started looking through the box of her things, but then couldn't continue. Not without my family.

When I'm finished, her expression is blank. "Wow."

"Yeah. I want Piper to come to Whitby for the show so I can talk to everyone. I meant to tell you all at once, but well . . ."

She reaches over and touches my arm with her palm. "I'm glad you told me. Thank you for trusting me with this." She pulls back. "I know I reacted badly when you told me about Aria."

I snort. "There's the understatement of the year."

She swallows. "I know. I was wrong. I lashed out at you because I felt guilty too."

My brows lift. "You did?" She might have mentioned her guilt before, the first time she apologized, but I was too pissed to listen.

"I never truly blamed you for what happened to Aria. You were only sixteen. I blamed myself."

"Why? You didn't even live here. You were off at college."

She blows out a breath. "Aria wanted to come stay with me that weekend. We had talked about it a few times before, her coming to visit for a night or two so she could check out the campus and hang in the dorms. And I kept blowing her off. I was too busy enjoying college life. And then she died." She blinks rapidly, holding back tears. "It was easier to be angry at you than to acknowledge my own culpability."

My tongue sticks to the roof of my mouth, shock stealing my voice.

"Then when you opened up about what happened, I was . . . resentful that you would share it with me. You had reached a point where you were ready to open up. But I hadn't. I didn't have the guts to face my own shame. Every time I looked at you after that, all I could see was my own guilt, my own fear, my own cowardice staring me in the face." Her eyes fall shut, tears tracking down her cheeks.

I can't stand it any longer. I lean forward and wrap my arms around her shaking shoulders. I felt the same way when she apologized to me last year. I couldn't even handle being home, because it reminded me that while she was able to move forward, forgive me, forgive herself and then push through the grief, I wasn't.

But maybe I'm getting there.

"I'm sorry," she says, between tears.

"I know."

She pulls back to wipe her eyes. "I'll make it up to you, I promise."

"Hell, yeah you will. You can start by helping me tell the rest of our family about Mom."

She chuckles. "Of course."

Relief crashes over me. "Thank you. Also, I might need your help getting Piper to visit while you're still here."

She nods without hesitation. "Of course. I'm on it."

I purse my lips. "And maybe you could clean the bathroom Jake and I have been sharing."

She rolls her eyes, pushing me on the shoulder. "Now you're just being greedy."

We laugh and memories flood through me, all the moments we shared before Aria died and things went south. Mindy was always the first one I called when I needed anything, before Finley, even. She was the person I turned to for everything. She was the first person I talked to about my guilt over Aria's death. She was *my* person, which is why her anger stung so deeply, and why her sudden apology was like a Band-Aid over a knife wound.

She leans toward me. "Can I ask why?"

I blink. "Why what?"

"Why did you search for her?"

I take another leap of faith and decide to face the truth about myself I've been avoiding. "I wanted to know why she left, because I wanted to know if I was like her."

Mindy rocks back slightly. "What do you mean, like her?"

"She left. I leave." I wave a hand in the air. "It's like what I do. I'm flakey and unreliable, you've said it yourself a thousand times."

She winces. "I was wrong. I was lashing out at you because of my own issues." She leans toward me, her eyes serious. "Taylor, you aren't her."

I swallow and avert my gaze to the corner of the bed. "How do you know?"

"Because you come back. You always come back. Sure, you might need to get out there for a bit, but you would never disappear entirely. You would never ghost your family. You aren't that person."

She's right.

I might leave, but I don't stay away. I'm running from myself, not the people who love me. I couldn't. I care about my family too much.

Maybe I've been asking the wrong questions. Maybe it's not about why Mom left, but about why I always need to leave. Why can't I just stay still? What am I running from, really?

She shifts on the edge of the bed, leaning closer. "You were pissed at me, and you still helped me with Luke. When Jake is going through a hard time, you drop everything and come home. You're trusting me now, giving me the gift of forgiveness, even though it's the last thing I deserve."

My lips tremble with a smile. "I've also given you the gift of many hostile family dinners."

She huffs out a laugh. "I think we're both guilty there. But seriously, Taylor, the fact you're even worried about being like Mom sets you light-years apart from her."

I swallow. "Thank you." Turning away, I clear my throat. "Anyway, no more sappy crap. Let's get down to business."

We spend some time going over the contract and payment details for the upcoming show.

"This is going to be great," Mindy says, shuffling the paperwork back into the file. "Thanks again for doing this. It's too bad you aren't staying longer. Veronica's would be the best outdoor venue if we had time to clean up the back and set up a stage. Can you imagine? She has all that space. It could be like Electric Forest or something. But on a much smaller scale, obviously."

It takes a few seconds for the words to sink in, but when they do, I'm thunderstruck by the idea, like a bolt of lightning from the AC/DC gods.

"I have a little bit of time," I say slowly. "The bus won't be done for another month. Would that be enough time to plan something like that? Like a one-day lineup . . . Veronica basically gave me free rein, but I would let her know for sure."

Mindy blinks. "I don't know. I guess it's possible if we could book the musical acts that quickly." She rubs her lips together, and then her eyes widen. "What if Outfoxed Records sponsors the event, and we do all or mostly acts from my label?"

My mind whirrs around the idea. "Would that even work?"

"I think so. If we do it three weekends from now, Luke could play too. I think at least six of my artists will be free then, but I'll have to check the calendar."

My heart pounds. Am I actually considering this? Can we really pull something off?

Mindy's eyes are bright, her face animated. "We have venue, musicians, and funding—which can be recouped through ticket sales. We can have the stage built on the east side of the property behind the building. Maybe we can do camping in the trees, there's a couple of flat meadows back there. Oliver has some connections where we could maybe get in some food trucks, in addition to the restaurant and the bar."

"We'll need a lot of staff, for tech setup and everything else. A few porta potties for sure."

Mindy grabs my hand. "This could be amazing. Everyone wants to get in on these things when they're small, before they turn into Burning Man and Coachella."

"What would we call it? Outfoxed Festival?"

Her eyes widen. "Really?"

"Well, yeah, especially if you're footing the bill."

She grins and reaches out, shaking my arm. "That would be incredible."

I continue taking notes as we throw out ideas.

"We could put up some tree tents and hammocks," Mindy says.

I jot it down. "Oh, what about yurts? Bonnie and Elliot have some nice ones they rent out."

She gasps. "That would be amazing."

I make another note. "What about getting local artists to help with decorating in the trees?"

"That is a great idea." Her eyes widen and she snaps her fingers. "We can see if Piper wants to help, maybe put her in charge. Then we can get her to Whitby while we're all here."

I nod slowly. "And she said she's had a bit of artist's block. Maybe this is a good chance for her to be creative in a different way."

"We could definitely sell it to her. Also, there are footpaths that wind through the trees. She could decorate along those, so when people move from the stage area to the camping area, there will be lights and art installations and whatever we want really."

I write faster and then turn around and grin at Mindy, excitement a beat in my veins. "I know a hundred people right now that would drop everything and come here right this minute."

She rubs her chin. "We'll have to cap the size."

I purse my lips, turning back to the notepad. "How much should we charge for the entry and camp fees?"

We throw out more ideas and then Mindy says, "We'll have to call Reed at the county office for the permits."

"You think he can push it through on a tight timeline?"

"I've known him since grade school, so he better."

"He also dated Finley so maybe we can get her to call him."

She makes a face. "I think she broke up with him for Archer."

"Maybe Jake can call him."

We laugh and then we're interrupted by a knock on the door.

"Hey." Finley stands in the doorway, her eyes flicking back and forth between us. "What's so funny?" She's smiling at us, the brightness in her face almost blinding. It's been a long time since Finley has looked so incandescently happy, at least when Mindy and I are in the same room together.

A weight lifts from my spine, leaving me nearly breathless. I knew our rift was affecting Finley, but until now I wasn't aware just how much.

I glance at Mindy and then grin at Finley. "I think we're starting a new family business."

CHAPTER
Twenty-Two

TAYLOR

"One of the food trucks needs a generator. Theirs died. I'm going to run to the camp and grab one of ours. And my tool belt because things keep falling apart." Jake finds me in the middle of attempting to defuse twelve million other explosions.

"Tell me about it," I mutter. Reed from the county office is around here somewhere. I need to find him to finalize all the permits for the event. I have to guide vendors where to set up to avoid any clashing if lines build up, and I've been showing staff where to place speakers, lights, hammocks, campsites, and the art pieces to spread throughout the nearby wooded area. All of that in between putting out one fire after another. But it will be worth it.

I can't wait until tonight to get a look at everything

we've been working on. It's been a rush all day to set it all up for the test run. Piper is overseeing the art in the woods, and Mindy has been coordinating all the artists' schedules.

The festival isn't until tomorrow, but we need everything in place before attendees begin arriving in the morning.

I return my attention to Jake's problem. "Maybe grab two generators, just in case. We can store one in Veronica's office."

"Good idea." He nods and then squints toward the stage to our left. "What are they doing?"

I follow his gaze. Archer and Atticus are assisting the event techs with carrying boxes full of cords and amps and who knows what else. They set down a long, heavy speaker at the end of the stage and high-five. "They're helping with the heavy stuff."

Jake frowns.

"Wait, are you jealous?" I ask.

"No," he scoffs.

Archer laughs at something Atticus says, throwing his head back in mirth.

"Fine. Maybe a little. They are a lot alike. Both big and brawny with names that start with A." He raises a hand in their direction. "Look at them. They're like carbon copy Paul Bunyans." He kicks the ground before trudging away.

I shake my head, blowing out a breath and turning to the next person who needs me, getting lost in my ever-increasing to-do list, a frenetic state that has become second nature over the past three weeks.

It's been a whirlwind of research, planning, phone calls, and delegating wherever I can.

Not to mention spending as much time as possible in between the madness with Atticus.

Almost every night, I sneak over and spend the night with him, each time more frenzied than the last.

After the show tomorrow night, I'm gone.

The parts for my bus came in earlier in the week, and I gave Pearl the okay to finish the work.

Maybe I should stay a little longer to save up for some travel funds.

Maybe I should stay, period. But then what will I do? Veronica is coming back. She doesn't need me indefinitely. If I'm going to stay in any one place, music has to be involved, and Whitby isn't exactly a mecca for . . . anything.

If I had some kind of opportunity to pursue, I might actually consider it.

After all, I've been home almost two months, the longest I've stayed home in years. I should be jumping out of my skin by now.

But I'm not.

By the time the sun is sinking down over the horizon, almost my entire to-do list has been accomplished —at least all the major things.

While walking back toward Veronica's, my phone chimes. I answer the call on the first ring, praying it isn't another problem to solve.

"Is this Taylor Fox?" a woman's voice asks.

"Yep, you got her." I wave at one of the staff passing in the opposite direction.

"My name is Kayley York. I'm calling from Silvertongue."

I push open the back door, freezing mid-step as I take in the statement.

"Silvertongue? The event organizers?"

They're huge. They do events all over the country, large and small. TuneFest, Cruel Summer, and Gingerbread Heads, to name a few.

"That's us. I hope it's okay that I'm calling. Mindy gave me your number. She said you might be interested in a position we're looking to fill."

Surprise tumbles through me. "A position?"

"We are looking for people just like you to run events on the West Coast."

Holy shit.

Sticking to the edges of the restaurant to avoid the dinner crowd, I make it into the office before I find the words to reply.

"You want me to run events?" I shut the door behind me and lean back against it, rolling my eyes at myself. "Sorry for the parrot routine, I'm just surprised."

Kayley chuckles. "No worries. I know Mindy may not have had a chance to fill you in."

She runs through a spiel that I only half listen to through the racing of my heart. This is like a dream.

"It's not an easy job. We are looking for motivated

people with knowledge of the music industry who aren't afraid to be creative and try new things. There will be a lot of traveling. I can send you the proposal if you want to look it over?"

I nod, and then nearly smack myself in the forehead. She can't see me. "Yes," I manage to get out. I rattle off my email and promise to call her within the next week and then hang up, in a bit of a daze.

This is everything I've ever wanted. Traveling to music festivals, working with musicians and people in the industry . . . how can I refuse?

A knock on the door behind me whacks me from my stupor.

I whirl around and yank it open.

"Hey." Atticus's palms rest on either side of the doorway. "Are you ready to check out Fox Forest? It's dark enough."

I take him in for a second, admiring the warmth in his eyes and the intrinsic strength in his frame.

How can I leave him behind?

I clear my throat, shoving those thoughts away. I'll deal with that later. "I'm ready."

We walk side by side, our fingers brushing occasionally as we pass through the bar and restaurant.

We exit out the back door. The sun has disappeared behind the surrounding mountains, the final rays splashing color across the errant clouds in the sky, setting the world aglow in oranges and pinks.

Some of the event staff lingers, doing final touches and cleanup.

There are multiple entrances into the woods behind Veronica's, each following a trail that weaves through the forest. All of the entry points have been framed with arches laced with fairy lights, like a portal into another world.

I clap my hands, rubbing them together. "I can't wait to see this."

"It was a good idea, enlisting Piper for the art exhibitions."

"It was Mindy's idea." And it was brilliant.

We pass under the nearest arch into the trees and I gasp.

Colorful lights twinkle from the trees, casting a warm glow over everything they touch.

Lanterns line the walkways, directing us deeper into the woods and shining over carefully placed artwork set alongside the trails, off the beaten path so they don't get tripped over.

Wood carvings as detailed as photographs are tacked onto tree trunks. Sculptures made from a variety of materials are set in intervals along the route, each one with a placard detailing the name of the piece and the artist.

I stop before one of the arrow-shaped wooden signs directing people to the Fox Den, which is what we decided to name the campground. "This is incredible."

Atticus glances down the curve of the trail before tugging me into the trees. I follow him willingly.

As soon as we're off the path, hidden by foliage, I throw myself into his arms.

We come together like we always do, an all-consuming explosion of lust and hunger tinged with desperation.

I lose myself in the welcoming heat of his arms, his taste, the rumbling sounds he makes when I suck on his tongue.

"I wish we could spend a whole night together." *Before I leave.* Our time is always so fleeting. Just once, I wish I could wake up in his arms, without having to get home before the sun rises.

His nose rubs against mine. "I'll make it happen." Then we come together again.

I can't think about how my heart will implode when it's over, so I focus on the slide of my fingers against the skin of his stomach, the press of his hand against the small of my back, and the scent of his skin mixed with the fresh pine air.

"Taylor?" Piper's voice rings through the trees, followed by a quieter murmur, "Are you sure you saw them come down this way?"

We freeze.

His hand is under my shirt, my fingers undoing the buttons on his pants.

We scramble to put our clothes back to rights.

"Come on." Atticus's voice is a low vibration against my ear before he grabs my hand, leading in the opposite direction from Piper's voice so we can circle back and come up behind her on the path.

"We have family dinner tonight," I tell him while we creep through the trees.

He squeezes my hand. "Tonight's the night, then?"

I blow out a breath. "Yep." The night I come clean to my family.

I have to admit, I'm not as nervous as I thought I would be. I have Mindy in my corner, backing me up since she's the only one besides Atticus who knows the truth.

He stops walking and cups my face in his warm palms. "You'll do great. They love you."

I clutch at his wrists, wishing we had more time. I could really use an earth-shattering orgasm right now to distract me from . . . everything. "I know."

"Taylor?" Piper's voice calls from the other side of the path, a clump of trees and bushes blocking her from view.

By silent agreement, we kiss one last time and I savor the sensation of his hands on my skin, his mouth on mine, absorbing every touch, every second we have left together.

I leave him for the path where Piper is calling, while he takes an alternate route back to Veronica's.

I make every effort to banish Atticus from my thoughts, to pretend the end of . . . whatever we are isn't looming on the horizon.

He crawled past all my defenses and burrowed into my heart. He makes me happy. He makes me burn. His mere presence wraps around me like a warm blanket on a breezy day.

A dark, achy feeling swamps me, but I shove it away and greet Piper with a smile.

CHAPTER
Twenty-Three

TAYLOR

Our dining room table has borne witness to a lot of things. Egg decorating at Easter, birthday parties, Thanksgiving, and a lot of family dinners where we laughed and fought and cried.

And now it's going to be a part of the conversation where I tell all my siblings our mother is dead.

Mindy and I came up with a game plan. After dinner, that's when I tell them, when everyone is eating pie.

No one can be mad when they're eating pie. Well, maybe they can, but Jake can't, so that's at least one of them.

The final slice has been plated and served when Mindy widens her eyes at me, and I open my mouth to speak.

"I have to tell you all something."

Startled, my gaze flies to Finley, who stole the words right out of my mouth. She bites her lip and fiddles with her fork.

I look over at Mindy. She lifts her brows and gives a subtle shrug.

What is this all about?

"Is it good news or bad?" Jake shoves a bite of pie in his mouth.

"Good. I think it's good, anyway. I hope you all do too." The fork slips from her hand, clattering against her plate.

Is she nervous?

Piper, sitting next to Finley, shifts closer. "You can tell us anything, you know that."

Finley nods, a smile playing around her lips. She takes a deep breath. "So, here's the thing. Archer proposed." When we've all sucked in a collective breath, she adds, "And I said yes."

The table erupts into chaos, everyone talking and laughing and pushing our chairs back to jump all over Finley.

She laughs when we finally step back. "One at a time, I can't even hear what you're saying."

Piper gets her question out first. "When's the wedding?"

Finley shrugs. "I'm not sure. We haven't gotten that far yet."

"How did he propose?" I ask.

"Well, uh . . ." She flushes and averts her eyes.

"Oh, gross." Jake grimaces. "We don't need the gory details."

Piper shushes him. "I want the gory details."

"Are you pregnant?"

"Jake!" We all yell at once.

Finley rolls her eyes. "No. I don't even know if we want kids. I already raised all you yahoos. Why would I want to do that again?"

Mindy smirks. "We turned out great. We're only slightly demented and trauma-ridden."

Jake leans his hip against the table. "My therapist says you're awesome. It's Mom who fucked us all up."

Mindy elbows me and clears her throat.

"I can't now." I mouth at her, gesturing with my hands.

"Can't what now?" Jake picks up his pie plate, shoving a giant forkful into his mouth.

My eyes dart to his in surprise.

"You're the loudest whisperer ever, Tay."

I shift on my feet. "Fine. I have something I need to tell you all too, but maybe we should wait until another time."

Mindy cocks her head to one side. "If not now, when?"

I blow out a breath. "Fine. Let's do it now. It tracks that we need to find some way to ruin a happy family moment I guess."

Mindy moves to step past me. "Do you want me to get the box?"

I nod.

Jake perks up. "A box? More pie?"

I grimace. "Sorry, Jake. It's not pie."

"Cake then? Donuts?"

"It's not food, Jake." Mindy squeezes my shoulder and then jogs up the stairs to grab Mom's stuff from under my bed.

Jake grumbles.

I sit back down and gesture, then wait for Finley, Piper, and Jake to take their seats. Mindy comes back downstairs, setting the box at the end of the table.

Might as well put it out there, like ripping off a Band-Aid. "Mom's dead."

Piper's jaw drops.

Finley's face goes slack. "How do you know?"

"I hired a PI to find her, and well, I did. At least, I found where she was living when she passed."

Jake rocks back in his chair. "It's not her in the box, is it?"

"Jake!" Piper smacks him on the shoulder.

He flinches. "What?"

She rolls her eyes and turns to me. "How? When?"

I take a deep breath and blow it out. "Two years ago. She had dementia."

Mindy returns, setting the boxes in the middle of the table. "These are her things. We haven't looked through them."

Finley's head whips toward Mindy. "You knew?"

"Only recently."

I swallow. "I should have told you all, but I—I don't

know, I thought you wouldn't approve, and I didn't want to say anything until I knew for sure.

I go through everything with them, finding the picture, hiring Georgia, how it led to Boylesville, Pennsylvania, Jonas and his mother, the whole story.

"She would talk about you, Finley. Near the end. But she had dementia and wouldn't say anything specific. And she saw Aria."

Piper's mouth drops open, Finley swallows, and Jake's face goes carefully blank.

"What do you mean?" Finley asks, her voice soft.

"She told Jonas that Aria had been there to visit and she was coming back for her. She died a week later."

A palpable silence hangs in the air, thick with the weight of the information I laid on them. When the fridge in the kitchen clatters from ice dropping in the ice maker, it may as well be the rumble of thunder.

Jake is the first to break. "That would be just like her, to show up for someone who didn't deserve her love or mercy."

Finley reaches over and grabs Jake's hand. "She was the best of us."

We're silent for a moment, recognizing the truth of the statement.

"I'm sorry I didn't say anything. I should have told you all sooner." I swallow, my mouth dry. "I have Jonas's card, so if anyone wants to talk to him, or has any other questions . . . Also I thought, since we went through Dad's things together, we could do this together too." I motion to the box Mindy set at the end of the table. "You know, if you want."

Piper's head tilts, angling toward Finley. "It's up to you." She looks over at Mindy. "And you. You both remember her the most."

Mindy glances over at me and then nods. "I'm in."

Everyone looks at Finley.

She blows out a breath. "I'm in this with all of you, of course."

We pop off the lid and everyone digs in, taking turns grabbing items out. We set aside some of them, like pay stubs and tax forms, and share others around the table, like photographs and old coins and jewelry, a smattering of old CDs, *Tristan und Isolde* and *Don Giovanni*.

"She used to be very erratic." Finley's voice startles me.

I look up. She's staring down at an empty prescription pill bottle in her hand.

"You remember that?" Piper asks.

Finley nods. "Sometimes she was so much fun. Exciting. Wanting to go on impromptu trips or taking me and Mindy to a surprise breakfast before school. Other times it was," she frowns, "scary."

"What do you mean?" I ask.

"She took us on a day trip to the city and we were gone until it got dark. Except she didn't call the school to let them know we would be out, and she didn't tell Dad. He was freaking out. They fought. She would scream, threaten," she swallows, "and blame us." She nods to Mindy.

I frown.

Piper speaks up before I can. "Wait. She blamed you? When you were what, five?"

"Six or seven, maybe. But yeah. She said we were crying to not go to school, and she was just trying to be a good mom." She shakes her head. "It wasn't true though."

My jaw tightens in annoyance on their behalf. "Even if it was, you were kids."

Finley's head tilts to one side. "Yeah, that's what Dad said. It set her off more. She took off, made him worry all day, and then somehow turned it around on him." Finley looks up and meets my eyes, a crease between her brow. "I'm sorry I didn't tell you more or talk about her more. Maybe I should have. It was hard for me to talk about her, to come to terms with the fact that she left. I thought it was my fault or something, but that's no excuse. I didn't know you felt the lack."

I stand up and walk over to her, bending over to throw my arms around her neck. "There was no lack. You were the best sister-mother a girl could ask for."

She laughs, the sound thick with emotion.

I'm not sure my search was about finding Mom at all. It was about finding myself.

I pull back, keeping my hand on her shoulder. "It's sad, actually, how much she missed, not knowing us."

Jake nods. "Right? I'm awesome."

Finley's troubled eyes glance around the table. "I got all the moments she lost. I was the one you snuggled with when you were sad. I got to share all your firsts, first days of school, first dates, first heartbreaks, and I got to hear all the silly things you said and did when you were little."

Piper taps her finger on the table. "Like how Jake made you wipe his butt until he was five?"

We all laugh.

Jake shrugs. "Seriously, that was an awesome time in my life. I'd pay for someone to wipe my ass for me now."

Mindy wrinkles her nose. "Gross. I don't remember very much about her. I remember her being sad sometimes, but that's about it. Oh, and the necklace."

My ears perk up. "Wait, the phoenix necklace?"

She nods, her brow furrowing in confusion. "Yeah, how did you know?"

"I've seen it." I move over to the box, digging into it until I find the necklace that slipped down to the bottom. "Here. You should have it."

"Are you sure?" She takes it from my outstretched hand and looks at it for a second, and then holds it up. "Does anyone else want it?"

"Maybe we can take turns, like the sisterhood of the traveling phoenix," Piper says.

Mindy hands it to her for inspection.

Jake pouts. "What about me?"

Finley narrows her eyes down at the necklace. "It is kind of masculine."

Jake puts out his palm. "Let me see. I'll wear something pretty, I don't care."

They continue talking, and Mindy squeezes my

shoulder, moving to my side to sort through more trinkets from the box.

For the first time in months, I take a deep breath. A giant weight that had been pressing on my shoulders, a heaviness disappears like a puff of smoke brushed away on a breeze.

I need to tell Atticus.

The urge washes over me like a tidal wave, powerful and fierce. More than anything, I want to share my relief, the good news, the offer from Silvertongue that I didn't tell him about earlier. There is no one else I'd rather be with, to share my triumphs and losses.

The thought is immediately followed by panic.

I'm an idiot.

I'm so in love with him.

CHAPTER

Twenty-Four

ATTICUS

"You made it." The brightness of Taylor's grin wraps around my heart and squeezes.

Tracking her down amongst the crush of people swarming the event was next to impossible, especially in the dark, despite the lights bouncing off the stage and dots of illumination lining the venue.

I finally locate her, far enough away from the stage that the music isn't quite as deafening, but close enough that there are people swaying and dancing nearby.

I've been working all day since we got a group of kids in yesterday and finally finished all the camper activities only an hour ago.

I spent the entire day distracted, wondering how things were going, hoping the plan I set up for us tonight would work out. I texted Taylor a couple of times, but I'm not sure she's had a chance to glance at her cell phone, let alone reply to texts. When I arrived, I had to ask a member of her staff, dressed in all black with one of those walkie-talkie earpieces, to help me narrow down her location.

"How has it been going?"

She grabs my arm. "It's incredible. I mean, it's exhausting, challenging, and I think my legs are going to pop right off my body because of how much I've been running around but look at this." She gestures around us. "I did this."

My gaze sweeps over the swaying crowd, the singer crooning on the stage, and all the people enjoying themselves, singing along, dancing, and laughing.

And I get it.

It's joy. It's exhilarating and extraordinary.

"You're incredible." I nudge her with my elbow.

Her smile is tender. "Thank you."

I step close enough that my chest brushes her shoulder. Reaching down, I discreetly squeeze her fingers and speak in her free ear, the one not covered by the earpiece. "I have a surprise for you."

Her smile widens. "You do?"

"Meet me by the Fox Den sign later, right off the path where we were yesterday?"

She nods, then winces and glances down at her illuminated watch. "It might be late. The last set starts in twenty."

"We've got all night."

Her eyes gleam. "Do we?"

"I ensured it."

Her eyes heat and she bites her lip.

My gaze zeroes in on the motion. We're in a crowd of people in the dark. Surely no one will notice if I take a little taste.

"Ace!" Jake slaps his hand on my back. "I see you found the star of the event."

I stifle a groan.

"What's up, Jakey?" Taylor moves away from me with a subtle shift, her fingers dropping from mine.

I ignore the pang in my chest. I know she isn't embarrassed by me, it's not about me at all, but the action still stings.

"I came to see if my good buddy here wants to check out the photo booth." He jerks a thumb behind him.

Taylor made use of some of the random items scattered around Veronica's as props, and the backdrop was special ordered with the Outfoxed logo splashed all over it. They included QR codes and hashtags on some surrounding banners to encourage posting to social media.

Taylor chuckles, shaking her head. "Laying it on a little thick here, aren't you?"

Jake puts a hand on his chest. "I have no idea what you mean."

She looks up at me. "He's jealous of you and Archer."

"I am not jealous. Now c'mon, Ace, let's go take

some pictures for the camp photo wall of me and my bestie." He grabs my arm, tugging me with him.

I shoot Taylor a glance as we walk away, and she nods, silently communicating we'll meet up later. My stomach dips. We only have a few more days until she leaves.

"We can take pics in the tub together," Jake says, snapping my attention back to him.

"What?" He wants to take a bath together?

"The porcelain tub." He points over to the white bathtub set inside the photo area. "Me and that tub have shared some special moments together." His voice is wistful.

I grimace. "Did they sanitize it?"

Jake laughs, overly loud. "You're hilarious. Come on, I want to text a pic of us to Archer before he goes to bed. By the way, I saw your aunt Moira earlier over by the porta potty smoking a joint with some hipster dude."

It's going to be a long, long, *long* night.

Taylor's arms slip around me from behind, her hands linking on my chest and squeezing me tight. "The stars are beautiful."

I spin around, tugging her against me before sliding my hands up the nape of her neck into her hair and covering her mouth with mine.

Her pulse flutters against my thumbs. I breathe her

in, wanting nothing more than to sink into her scent, into the whisper of her fingertips trailing up my back, and the ardent way she returns my kiss like she's starved for it.

But not quite yet. "Come on." I pull away, linking her hand in mine and leading her through the dark woods, a faint glow coming from the stars gleaming overhead and some of the overflow illumination winding into the trees from the lights on the trail.

It's after two a.m. The night air is cool, and the forest is mostly quiet, except for the occasional burst of laughter and the sift of conversation floating on the breeze from the direction of the camps, people still winding down even though the music ended two hours ago.

Her hand squeezes mine. "Are we going back to my tent?" Her space was set up farther into the trees, away from the main camps.

"You'll see." I took the liberty of switching out her smaller, three-person shelter for a larger, slightly more extravagant version. Most of the work was done last night, while she was having dinner with her family. More was added tonight, with the assistance of one of the techs who promised to keep it to himself.

She skips, bouncing slightly ahead of me. "Ooh, I love surprises." Even in the shadows, her eyes gleam with excitement.

A few minutes later, the dim glow of battery-powered lanterns I placed on either side of the tent door comes into view.

She gasps and halts in her tracks. "What is this? This is different. This wasn't here yesterday." She peers up at me, eyes wide. "You did this?"

A smile tugs at my lips. "Come on." I pull her inside.

The circular tent is broad enough that it can easily sleep ten. In one corner, a queen-sized cot is loaded with pillows and blankets. Next to it is a cooler with drinks and snacks. In the opposite corner rests an inflatable hip bath. Lights are strung around the ceiling, casting a light glow over everything.

She freezes in the doorway, taking in the space. "Is that a bath?"

"I have to warn you, it was warm an hour ago so it might be—"

She whips her shirt over her head.

My mouth goes dry.

"It could be an ice bath for all I care, I have been sweating all day." She keeps yanking off clothes, her pants joining her shirt on the floor, and then her bra and underwear.

Completely unselfconscious, she saunters over to the tub, climbing in and sinking down into the water with a sigh.

Once her delicious curves are immersed, she gives me a saucy wink. "Are you going to just stand there, or are you going to help me wash my hair?"

I stumble in my haste to reach her and she releases a peal of laughter that shoots straight to my cock.

Thirty minutes later, we're lying on the bed. She's

snuggled into my arms and I'm breathing in her hair.

"That was the best bath I've ever had."

"Me too."

She chuckles, propping herself up on an elbow to rub her lips against mine. "Thank you."

"For what?"

She gestures to the tent. "Everything." Her gaze drops, her fingers making aimless circles against my skin, fidgeting with the tree of life necklace against my chest.

She always does that when she's anxious.

"What is it?"

Her eyes lift to mine. "I have to tell you something."

I squeeze her a little tighter. "You can tell me anything."

Her smile is sad. "I know." Her fingers still, hand curling into a fist. "I got a call yesterday from Silver-tongue. They're a company that coordinates music events all over the country. They offered me a job."

Excitement on her behalf flashes through me. "That's great news."

"It involves traveling. And it's for their West Coast venues."

So far away.

My heart twists, but I shove the entirely selfish emotion to the side. I search her eyes, trying to gauge her reaction. "Is it great news?"

After a moment's hesitation, she nods. "It is. It's something I would love to do, and I never thought I would be given a chance like this, to have a job doing something so close to my heart. But it's on the other side of the country."

Stay.

The word catches in my throat. I can't ask her to change her life for me. I can't ask her to give up the opportunity of a lifetime—to work in music, a dream job, her heart's desire—and instead to set down roots for me. What if she became resentful and miserable? It would be my fault.

What if I went with her? How could I ask? She told me this is a temporary fling. But surely her feelings are as involved as much as mine. Maybe I could return to my work in field botany, but I couldn't be sure I would end up wherever she was. And if she's traveling up and down the West Coast regularly . . . I try to find a path forward, but every route leads me in a circle that results in a dead end.

She deserves to live the life she wants.

I shift my head to look at her more fully. "I want you to be happy, Taylor."

She blinks and nods. "I know." Then she leans forward and her lips press against mine, her hands smoothing up my chest to my shoulders.

Want and fear swing through me, yanking me in opposing directions. The kiss is equal parts tender and frantic. She nips at my lip and then soothes it with her tongue, shooting lust through my body.

This woman.

I flip us over, coming between her legs and aligning our bodies with practiced ease. Keeping my eyes fixed on hers, our fingers entwined on either side of her head, I slide into her slick warmth. The urge to slam into her and take her quickly, over and over, burns through me, almost impossible to deny. But not tonight. Tonight is for worshipping.

So I proceed to do just that.

CHAPTER
Twenty-Five

TAYLOR

For the first time this summer, I wake up to the sun shining and Atticus's arms wrapped around me.

Unlike the last time we spent a full night together back in December, I don't have the urge to sneak away. I could lie here forever, actually, drinking in the press of his skin against mine, the smell of his cologne, and the slow thump of his heart under my cheek.

Last night was incredible. Sex with Atticus is always fantastic, but it was different this time. More intense, more desperate. He worked me with his hands, with his cock, until we were both drunk on the need for release. He shoved me over the edge with the plunge of his tongue in my mouth, licking and nipping while he rode me in long strokes.

He twisted me into knots and then wrung me out to

dry, then held me tenderly, his fingertips stroking against my skin in lazy circles like he never wanted to stop.

It made my chest ache.

When I told him about the job, he didn't ask me to stay. I don't know if I appreciate that he's not pressuring me or if I'm pissed he didn't try harder to keep me.

Of course he didn't. He wants me to be happy, and he thinks this job will make me happy, and it will. Won't it?

The thought of leaving cleaves me into pieces, but I can't tether myself to Whitby because of a guy. Can I? What if I were to give up the job, stay here to be with him, and then we don't work out? What then?

When I inevitably return home to visit my family, we'll cross paths. He works at the camp. I won't be able to avoid him.

And I won't be able to touch him, taste him, breathe him in like I'm doing right now.

I've never been in a serious relationship. I'm probably going to screw something up at some point.

I'll have to stand by while he moves on with someone else.

The thought twists in my stomach, making me physically ill.

What's the alternative though, never coming home? Impossible.

Every potential path rolling out in front of me looms like a craggy mountain that's impossible to ascend.

"Are you okay?" His voice is husky with sleep.

I lift my head to meet his sleepy-eyed gaze. "Did I wake you?"

"Not really. But I can feel your tension."

"I'm sorry."

His arm clasps me tighter. "No need to be sorry." The worried crease between his eyebrows is so cute. I stretch up to kiss it.

Something clatters outside the tent.

"What is that?"

I twist toward the tent door right as the zipper slides down and Jake sticks his head inside. "Taylor, you awake yet? It's almost ten—oh Jesus." His head disappears, the zipper still half down.

I tuck my head into Atticus's neck, shoulders shaking with laughter. I turn my head to call out, "Jake, I told you, you need to learn how to knock."

There's no reply for a few long seconds, then he replies in a tortured voice, "This is a tent, there's nowhere to knock." He releases a long-suffering sigh. "Ace, please tell me you are both fully dressed under those blankets and there's a logical reason for the spooning that doesn't involve you boning my sister?"

I scramble out of bed and fumble for my clothes, dragging my T-shirt over my head.

Atticus sits up in the bed, making no moves to get dressed. "I can neither confirm nor deny our nudity and or the boning situation."

Jake groans. "Gross, man. We're best friends. I'm so hurt." He doesn't sound very hurt, actually.

I yank my pants up and then pull the zipper on the tent the rest of the way down. "It's fine Jake."

He leans against a tree trunk nearby. "I know. Trust me, I've seen way worse from our sisters." Then he waggles his finger at me. "You've been keeping more secrets, Taylor."

I sigh. "This isn't anyone's business except me and Atticus, Jake."

He stands up, shoving his hands in his pockets. "You're right."

I freeze. "I'm sorry, can you repeat that? And hold on, I'm going to grab my cell phone and record it."

He waves a hand at me. "I just wanted to let you know people are packing up to leave. The cleanup crew is here, and the stage is being dismantled." He kicks at the dirt, ducking his head and lowering his voice. "And if you and Ace are happy, I'm happy. He's a great guy. You've done way worse."

I chuckle and then glance over my shoulder at Atticus, lying in the rumpled sheets we shared last night, hands behind his head, body like a Greek god.

My stomach dips.

Leaving is really going to suck.

The next three days are a whirlwind. I blink and Veronica returns, full of stories about her new precious grandbaby, delighted about how our little musical festival went off without a hitch. And my bus is fixed and ready to take me on to the next adventure.

I made enough in earnings and the proceeds from the festival to fund the repairs to the bus and then some.

My family is surprisingly chill when Jake spills the beans about Atticus and me. Maybe because I'm leaving and anything that might be between us is over before it begins. Maybe because they know me, and my longest relationship thus far has been with a bottle of wine.

Yep. That's me. Noncommittal, go-with-the-flow, breezy Taylor.

Is it, though? Am I still that person?

"You'll be home before Thanksgiving, right?" Finley asks, stepping back from our goodbye hug, her hands on my shoulders.

"Yeah. I'll call you."

We're standing outside the main house, next to my bus. It's all packed up, the tank is full, and I'm ready to head out to Silvertongue headquarters in Sacramento.

Jake is the next to tug me into an embrace. "Drive safe. Call when you can. Don't do drugs. Oh, and don't ever lie to me ever again."

I squeeze him tight. "I promise. And you too, baby brother."

Mindy left yesterday to meet up with Luke at his next tour stop. She was beyond excited about my new job, jumping up and down and squealing like a banshee when I gave her the news. I joined in her glee, ignoring the sinking in my stomach at the thought of leaving. I said my goodbyes to Archer this morning before he left to take care of camp duties, along with Atticus.

I stayed the night at Atticus's last night. We made slow, torturous love, wringing orgasms out of each other like it was our life's mission. I didn't sleep. He didn't either. In between bouts of sex, we lay together, not speaking, only touching and thinking.

We drove here together this morning, the drive drenched in the silence of unspoken words. What is there to say? It's not like we're breaking up, we were never together. Not really. This was just a fling.

I hate this. I hate everything about it.

But hey, I have a great new job.

Why isn't the thought as exciting as it should be?

Jake lifts his brows at me.

"What?" I ask.

He jerks his head to the side and looks pointedly at something over my shoulder.

I turn around.

Atticus is standing behind me, by the bumper of the bus, his hands shoved in his pockets.

Finley pats my shoulder as she passes, Jake following behind her up into the house, giving us our moment.

My heart thumps so loudly in my ears, their retreating footsteps barely register. "Hi."

"Hey." His gaze lifts to mine, dark torment shining in his eyes. "I hate this."

Unable to withstand the pull of his presence, I take a

few quick steps and then my face is pressed against his chest, his arms wrapped around me.

My throat burns. I never wanted to stay in Whitby. The thought of living in this small town for the rest of my life always made me ache to bolt. It was akin to a prison sentence.

Then why is this so hard? Why is my heart ripping itself into little pieces?

I tip my head back, and like he plucked the intention from my mind before it fully formed, his mouth is already there.

The kiss is wild, abandoned, and reeking of desperation.

Abruptly, he yanks away.

I'm left with my arms empty, half raised in his direction.

"I'm sorry." His breathing is heavy. His face, usually as readable as a book, is carefully blank. Closed off. Shutting me out. "I wish you every happiness." Then he spins around and stalks away.

Blindly, I get inside my bus, sitting in the driver's seat, trying to catch my breath and push down the tornado of emotion clawing through my chest.

I have somewhere to go. My dream job starts in a week. My life has never been better.

Then why is anguish searing through my veins, as if everything that truly mattered is over?

CHAPTER
Twenty-Six

ATTICUS

Taylor's been gone for three days, four hours, and fifteen minutes, but the hole in my chest hasn't decreased in the slightest, despite Jake's best efforts.

I frown down at the fabric in my hand. "Are you sure this is going to help?"

"Not at all. Will you pass me the purple thread?"

I reach over to the side table and hand him the spool, then turn back to the piece I'm working on. It's supposed to be a heart but it looks more like a lumpy, jagged rock.

Appropriate.

We're in the living room, working on cross-stitch. Finley and Archer are out to dinner at Veronica's. Paul and Moira are off for parts unknown and I couldn't handle another night staring at the couch where Taylor and I began, or the bed where it ended, so I stupidly agreed to this "super fun activity" with Jake.

Moira offered to postpone their travels, but I insisted they not change their plans for me, and this time I meant it. I work all day, and I can't stand being home at night, so I'm not much fun to be around. They've called and texted every day to check in on me.

He reaches into the bowl of popcorn on the coffee table, popping a couple kernels in his mouth and chewing. "I'm just really glad there's finally someone more messed up than I am. It's nice to be the caretaker, instead of the caretake-ee."

A small laugh huffs out of me.

"See." He points at me. "The activities are working already. That almost sounded like a laugh. Let me see your cross-stitch."

I turn it toward him.

He winces. "Man, you suck. I'm making this one for you. The words are done, I just need to add some flowers for the border." He holds it up and reads it out loud at the same time. " 'Get your shit together.' "

I sigh.

"You can hang it in your bathroom," he adds with a satisfied grin.

We work in silence for a few minutes. It's not that I don't appreciate what Jake's doing, because I do, but it's not working.

The job helps. The kids are distracting, but the Fox

family is not. Every time I'm with Jake and Finley, I'm reminded of Taylor's eyes, the shape of her mouth, and the sound of her laugh.

In two weeks, I'm taking a weekend off to meet Paul and Moira in Stony Point for golf. Maybe by then, the searing torment will have settled into a dull burn.

The side door in the kitchen creaks open. "Jake," Finley's voice calls out. "Are you home? You'll never believe what Veronica said." Footsteps clatter through the house, Finley's tread followed by Archer's louder clomp. "She wants to retire and move closer to her son so she called Taylor to offer to sell her the bar and—oh, Atticus. Heyyyy." She smiles at me, but it's halfway to a grimace.

They've been very careful about not mentioning Taylor around me. I'm sure they've talked to her. I've been tempted to call her myself, my thumb hovering over the Empress of Awesome listing in my contact list.

"It's okay," I tell Finley. "She's your sister, you can talk about her." But my heart is racing at her words. Veronica offered to sell Taylor the bar? What did she say? Is she coming back?

What if she turned Veronica down?

My emotions swing wildly from ecstatic hope to doubtful fear.

Finley and Archer exchange a glance, and then Finley makes her way into the living room, perching between Jake and me on the sofa. Archer folds his frame into the recliner facing us.

"So," Jake asks. "What did Taylor say?"

"I don't know." Finley clasps her hands in her lap. "Veronica got her voicemail. Her phone is probably dead. Again."

"Ace, you should go after her." Jake pokes his needle through his fabric, his gaze fixated on his work.

I grip the embroidery frame in my fingers so hard, the wood creaks. "What do you mean?"

"Did you ask her to stay?" Finley angles toward me.

Setting my cross-stitch on the coffee table, I lean back on the sofa. "No. I couldn't."

"Did you want her to stay?"

I scrub my hand through my hair in frustration. "Of course. But I couldn't ask her to give up her dreams for me. I want her to be happy."

Jake huffs. "I'm pretty sure she's as miserable as you are, my dude."

Miserable? "Are you sure?"

"Oh yeah," Jake says.

"Definitely," Finley says at the same time.

Hope curls around my heart. I could go after her. But then what? What if I show up and she doesn't want me there? What if they're wrong? What if she's already moved on?

I swallow. "What if she says no?"

Finley and Jake exchange a glance.

Finley reaches over and pats my knee. "At least then you'll know you tried."

She's right. If I don't try, if I don't at least ask her to stay, as selfish as it might be, I'll regret it forever.

I've already regretted every moment since she left.

Jake reaches around Finley and smacks my shoulder. "Go get our girl."

CHAPTER
Twenty~Seven

TAYLOR

I'm in Reno when I finally get a chance to charge my cell phone and return all the calls and messages I've missed.

"You want to sell Veronica's?"

In her voicemail, she said she wanted to talk. I thought maybe she had a question about the new filing system, not that she wanted to retire and offer me the opportunity to purchase Veronica's from her.

"It's time for me to move. Past time, really. When I was with my son and his family, I realized I didn't want to miss out on the little one growing up."

I stare out the windows of the bus at the broadside of a white casino towering nearby. I stopped at an RV park for the night. I wanted a little rest and a little time to sort through all of the tumultuous emotions twisting through me. "I-I have to think about it."

"Of course, honey, take your time. I know this might be the worst timing since you just started your new fancy job and all that. But I know how much you love this place. You're like family to me, Taylor. I needed to make sure you didn't want Veronica's before I sell it off."

"Thank you, Veronica. It really means a lot to me that you would ask."

She clears her throat. "How is it going, by the way? With the new job?"

I rub my head. "Fine. It's fine. Yeah, it's great." I inject enthusiasm into my voice.

"That's good, isn't it?" Confusion and concern coil around the words.

I'm confused too. And angry. And terrified. "It is good. Listen, I have to go, but I'll call you by the end of the week with an answer, I promise."

"Okay, sweetie, no rush. You take care, okay?"

We hang up and I slump back in the seat. *What am I doing?*

I spent the last week going through orientation at Silvertongue headquarters. It wasn't exactly like I thought it would be.

Everything was so . . . corporate. Lots of meetings, people in suits, paperwork, and formalities. Sure, that might change once I'm on the road, in the trenches.

The work I did at Veronica's, like for the festival, was small time, sure, but it was an opportunity to help artists that hardly anyone knows about. Bringing attention to musicians who would go unnoticed otherwise. Silvertongue only works with big names. It's an incredible opportunity, it's just not for me.

Not to mention, I've been miserable since I left Whitby. There's a hole in my heart and it's shaped like Atticus.

I quit before the week was out. I couldn't stay. The urge to bolt was back, biting at my nerve endings and I had to leave.

Now I don't know what to do with myself. I want to go back to Whitby, but anxiety is making me freeze up in confusion.

What if Atticus doesn't want me? He didn't ask me to stay. He didn't even try. He wants me to be happy, even if it's not with him.

I'm so angry I want to scream. How dare he be so noble and wonderful and caring?

I hate him.

But that's the problem, isn't it? I don't hate him. Not in the slightest.

I've spent every minute of every day since I left dwelling on my past, examining every minute of my interactions with Atticus and how Aria's death, my subsequent guilt, and then the whole fight with Mindy has impacted me over the past eight years.

I've been searching the country looking for answers, for peace, and running from my problems, but I can't find solace in the middle of a festival.

The truth is I've been running like a coward, trying

to escape from my past. But I can't run from myself. Everything I'm evading, good and bad, is a part of me whether I like it or not.

It's time to stop and face myself, and accept myself.

The horror.

The phone rings in my hand, startling me out of my thoughts. My heart leaps for a second, as it does every time I get a call or text.

Atticus?

Nope.

Jake. I swipe my thumb to answer.

"Hey, Jakey."

"Hey there, Tay-tay, whatcha doing?"

I'm running, again. I just don't know if I'm running away from something or running toward it.

"Not much." Just questioning all my life choices. "Everything okay?"

"Yeah, it's fine. I was just checking in. Oh, and I need you to settle a bet I have with Archer. They put you up at the Hyatt in downtown Sacramento, right? Not the Marriott?"

I frown. That's a weird bet. Then again, Archer and Jake fight over what constitutes a sandwich, so maybe not so strange. "I was at the Hyatt," I say carefully. I promised him no more lies.

"*Was* at the Hyatt? What does that mean? Where are you now? Are you okay?"

I roll my eyes at his increasingly panicked voice. "Calm down. I'm fine. I'm in Reno."

"I'm sorry, did you say Reno? What are you doing in Reno?"

Sighing, I slump back further in my seat, staring at the minifridge in the back of the bus. "I turned down the job with Silvertongue."

Shocked silence greets that little pronouncement.

"Jake? You still there?"

"Wha—who—why would you—are you coming home?"

And isn't that the one-million-dollar question? "I'm not sure. Maybe I'll stay here for a little bit." Gamble away my life, pan for gold in Virginia City, maybe bum around in Tahoe for the rest of the summer, who's to say? Although none of that is appealing at the moment.

He's quiet again, the line so noiseless I sit up straighter. "Jake? Did I lose you?"

"No. Sorry. I'm here. How far is Reno from Sacramento?"

"I don't know, like two hours or so."

"Huh. Okay. So . . . where exactly are you? In Reno, I mean. Where are you staying? Just in case we need to get ahold of you, or Finley asks, or there's an emergency, or, you know, whatever."

I frown. "Why are you being weird?"

"I'm not being weird." The pitch of his voice goes up three octaves. "I just need to know these things in case Archer tries to bet me again."

I roll my eyes. Whatever. "I'm staying at the RV park at the Grand Sierra."

"Okay. All right. Cool. Cool cool cool, look I gotta go, Taylor, I'll text you later, K bye."

The phone goes dead. I stare down at it.

What the heck was that all about?

Three hours later, I'm walking back to the bus from the hotel's pool. I'm carrying my clothes in one hand, a towel wrapped around my waist, still in my bathing suit. The sun set an hour ago, but it's still hot outside. I thought a swim would help me cool off or clear my head.

It didn't work. I'm off-kilter. It's like I'm stuck in one of those dreams where everything is familiar and yet not, like a mirror image of reality.

There is only one certainty in my heart. I love Atticus. I've never loved anyone, not like this. I can't let it go. I need to go home. I need to see him. Maybe then I'll find some clarity.

I glance up, and then stagger to a halt.

A large figure sits at the picnic table next to my VW, his eyes fixed on me.

My heart tumbles in my chest. The incongruity of the world around me wavers and flips then resettles and suddenly makes sense.

I burst into tears.

Two seconds later, familiar arms wrap around me, along with the scent of soap and cedar. "Hey," he murmurs into my hair. "I'm sorry. I'm so sorry."

I shove out of his embrace. "You should be sorry." I swipe at my eyes. "Why did you let me leave? Why didn't you ask me to stay? Why didn't you fight for us?" Each question gets louder and louder.

"Because I love you," he bursts out. "And I can't be the reason you're unhappy." His voice cracks on the last word.

I stare at him, stunned.

He swallows. "I don't want to be the reason you stay if it makes you miserable."

My face crumples. "I'm miserable without you." I throw my arms around him, dropping my clothes to the concrete and stretching up to press my mouth to his.

Without hesitation, he wraps me up, our lips moving in tandem like they didn't just spend over a week apart.

I hold his face in my hands, pulling back to look into his eyes. "You're really here."

"I'm really here."

"You look like shit." His scruff is longer than normal, his eyes red-rimmed, hair messy, shirt wrinkled.

He huffs out a laugh. "You look incredible."

My head tilts to one side. "You're a terrible liar. How did you find me?"

"Jake." His hands rub up my arms, sliding to my neck, his fingers stroking against the side of my face, his eyes dazed like he can't quite believe he's touching me.

"Jake? Oh. Yeah, that weird conversation makes more sense now. But I just talked to him a few hours ago. It would have taken you way longer to fly out here from Whitby."

"I drove here from Sacramento."

My mouth pops open. "Why were you in Sacramento?"

He bites his lip. "I was looking for you. I had to rent a car and make the drive after Jake called to tell me where you were."

My brows fly up. "What would you have done if I wanted to stay in California?"

"I would have asked if you had any space in your bus for me."

Stunned, I stare at him. "You would leave Camp Aria, your family, all of it, for me?"

His dark eyes search mine. "Taylor, I can't even begin to describe what I would do for you."

With a startled cry, I kiss him again, running my hands up his chest, and then down to his waist. It's not enough. I wrench away to drag him over to the bus, grateful I left the bed down and invested in curtains for the windows.

Frantic, we undress each other. The only sound is the whisper of our clothes hitting the floor and our panting breaths.

His hands delve into my hair, tilting my head while he ravages my mouth, taking me apart and then piecing me back together, and still, it's not enough.

"I need you inside me." I lie back, tugging him with me.

He shifts over me, arms braced on either side of my

head, his blunt head pressing against my entrance. His mouth sips at mine as he pushes inside, hard and insistent.

Yes.

I grip at his lower back, pressing at him, rocking my hips to drive him deeper, but he's in no hurry, sinking into me one inexorable inch at a time. His powerful frame trembles with leashed force as he sinks the full way in, lifting his head up to meet my gaze.

We shudder together, grasping at the moment like it might slip away. My hands glide up his body to close around his nape.

His eyes are raw, possessive, full of primal heat scorching me from the inside out.

Then we move, our bodies rocking in unison, a slow and tender dance. He lifts one hand to brush against my skin, cupping my breast, drawing circles around the sensitive peaks.

I lift my legs and lock them around him. Minutes later, pleasure ripples through me without warning, a wave that crashes into him and sucks him under, both of us groaning in the aftermath of release.

When I return to my body, I'm splayed on top of Atticus, clutching at his tree of life necklace like it's a lifeline, a rope tethering me to him.

"Are you hungry?" His chest vibrates under my cheek as he talks.

My stomach growls.

He chuckles. "Do you have any food in here?"

"Peanut butter and jelly okay?" I ask.

"That sounds perfect."

A smile tugs at the corner of my mouth. "How many?"

He shrugs. "A million."

I full-out laugh. "Did you just quote me back to me?"

"I may have."

I smack him on the chest. "I've got it covered this time." I hop up, completely naked, and take one step to get to the kitchen, opening the cupboard and pulling out the bread and peanut butter.

He props himself up on an elbow to watch, his eyes drowsy and heated.

I may or may not intentionally drop some of the jelly on my naked body, which delays the meal for about an hour.

Once we've both eaten, satisfied in more ways than one, we're snuggling in bed in the dark, reacquainting ourselves with the feel of each other with slow, lingering touches.

I prop myself up, resting my chin on his chest. "Do you have to go back to Whitby soon, or can you take a little bit of time?"

His eyes search mine. "I don't know. I'll have to call Finley. Why, what did you have in mind?"

I fiddle with the chain of his necklace. "I thought maybe we could drive back together. The bus is kinda slow though, so you may need to ask for the week off."

Under my fingertips, his heart rate speeds up. "How

long do you think you'll stay home? In Whitby, I mean?"

"Oh, I don't know, I was thinking maybe somewhere along the lines of . . . forever?"

After a weighty pause, he springs into movement, flipping me onto my back and coming over top of me. "Are you sure? You don't want to travel?"

"I mean, I'll definitely want to take some trips here and there. I've seen every corner of the US, but it might be cool to spend a week in Prague or a month in Italy, sometime in the future, you know, after I've saved up money and whatnot."

His head drops to my shoulder, and he takes a deep breath. "Are you sure?"

I lift my hands, cupping his cheeks and tilting his head to lock our eyes. "I might be if you'd be willing to extend this whole fling we have going on. I could use a travel companion."

He blinks rapidly. "Yes." The word emerges on a croak, followed by his mouth descending on mine.

Long minutes later we come up for air.

"I love you, Empress of Awesome. Wherever you want to go, I will follow."

I grin up at him. "We need to think of a good name for you too. Hmmm." I tap my chin. "I love you too, Emperor of My Heart."

He grimaces. "That was the cheesiest thing I've ever heard."

A laugh bursts out of me. "I don't know, I thought it was pretty good."

"We are definitely coming up with something else." He dips his head, sucking on the skin at my neck, his nose brushing against my skin.

"Later," I murmur, as pleasure zings along my nerve endings. "We'll do that later."

We tumble into desire together and it dawns on me that he may be my greatest adventure yet.

Epilogue

EIGHT MONTHS LATER

Taylor

The sky is cerulean blue, stretching to the horizon and punctuated by a smattering of fluffy white clouds. The turquoise sea mirrors the boundless sky. Gentle waves lap at the pristine white sand beach.

I could stare at this view forever.

Atticus pops up about thirty feet offshore, swimming toward the sand before climbing out of the ocean and stalking toward me. Water drips down his broad shoulders and chest, his swim trunks sticking to his muscled thighs.

I push myself up on my elbows to get a better look.

Yep. I could definitely gaze at this for eternity.

When he's within shouting distance, I wrinkle my nose. "You're blocking the view."

He stops in front of me, bends over to rip his shorts off before chucking them at me, the wet fabric thwacking me in the face and upper chest. Laughing, I slap the trunks down into the towel and then take him in.

Wowza.

He's buck naked and slicked with water and completely shameless.

And mine.

My mouth goes dry.

The water must be warm.

"I'm really glad this beach is deserted." My voice is husky, my eyes fixated on the giant hunk of man looming above me.

"Me too." He drops beside me, stretching out on his back, blocking the bright sun with a forearm slung over his eyes.

We're in Antipaxos, off the coast of Greece. We took the ferry from Corfu and then decided to stay for a couple of days and explore the island. The better to find a secluded little slice of heaven where we can fulfill one of my other bucket list items.

I shift to my side, drinking him in, hand clenching on the towel.

It's a game we've been playing throughout our entire vacation: who will jump the other person first? I can't give in *too* easily, but the beauty of the game is even if I lose, it's still winning.

This whole trip has been a dream come true, two sun-filled, idyllic weeks exploring Greece and surrounding islands.

Atticus informed me just last week he would be taking me somewhere, refused to detail where, and ensured everything at Veronica's would be taken care of while we were gone. He insisted on paying for everything, despite my protests, since Moira and Paul had invested all the money he was paying them in rent for years and he needed to do something good with the money.

The past eight months have been a whirlwind. I bought Veronica's. I was able to obtain a decent loan since Veronica's is an established business already churning out a profit, which has only gotten better and better each month with the inclusion of the live music every Saturday night. I also joined forces with Mindy to put on a semiannual music festival featuring only Outfoxed artists.

It's a lot of work, but it's fun and fulfilling and I'm happy. I get to see my family more often. I get to wake up with Atticus every day.

Atticus, who is currently doing his best to ignore me, even though I'm pressed against his side and only wearing two little scraps of barely-there fabric.

I sit up and reach behind my back, tugging at the strings of my top. "I can finally get rid of my tan lines." I slide the straps down my arms, reaching over to let the fabric whisper over his abs, enjoying the corresponding flex of his muscles before I toss the bikini next to his shorts.

"I'm not looking." The words are pressed between his clenched teeth. His eyes are squeezed shut, his fists clenched at his side.

"Hmm. That's too bad. You know, I think I should rub on some sunscreen. I don't think burned nipples would be a great look. Or feel, for that matter." I reach over for my bag, making as much noise as possible while I squeeze the bottle and then spread the lotion on with a groan. "Oh, that's nice."

It starts with a low rumble, emanating from his chest and increasing in volume as my moaning gets more and more exaggerated.

With a muttered curse, he finally concedes, rolling in my direction and sweeping me down, coming over top of me and nuzzling into my neck, one hand coming up to cover my breast.

So predictable.

"I win." Smug, I tilt my head to allow him better access.

His thumb brushes over my nipple. "Me too," he murmurs against my skin.

I shiver when he nips at my sensitized flesh, despite the sun beating down on us.

We get lost in the wild rush of desire. The roar of my pulse drowns out the lap of the waves against the shore and the buzz of insects in the shrubbery hugging the narrow slice of beach.

The afternoon stretches around us. The sun has

descended to a different angle by the time we collapse next to each other on the towel, our breathing ragged, bodies satisfied.

His fingers lace with mine. "Wow."

"Yep." Every time with Atticus is incredible. Sometimes it's sweet, sometimes it's intense, but it's always epic. Except . . . "I think I have sand in weird places."

Atticus chuckles, lifting my hand to kiss the back of it. "Well, we can't have that."

We rinse our bodies in the warm waters of the Ionian Sea, splashing around and playing until we're both tired and famished from the exertions.

Strolling back in the direction of our rented villa while the sun sets, we stop to eat a leisurely dinner on the patio of a seaside café before turning in for the night.

We shower off the exertions of the day, and then laze around on the couch, Atticus on one side, me on the other with my feet in his lap. His giant, warm hands envelop my toes, his thumbs rubbing my heels.

Heaven. Pure heaven.

Until my phone rings.

"I've got it." Atticus sets my feet to the side and pushes off the couch, taking two steps over to the mini kitchen, where my phone is resting on the counter. "It's Finley."

I sit up, glancing over at the clock. It's early afternoon in New York. I hold out my hand and he passes me the phone.

"Finley? Is everything okay?"

"Taylor, I'm so sorry to bother you on your vacation." Her voice is tight with tension.

My stomach drops. "What's going on? Is everything okay?"

"Everything is fine," she says quickly. "I mean I think it's fine. It's just, it's Jake."

My eyes lock with Atticus. A divot forms between his brows.

I shrug at him and ask Finley, "What do you mean? What's going on with Jake?"

She sighs. "I was hoping you would be able to tell me. He always talks to you more than me. He tells me I worry too much."

"Finley, what is it?"

She blows out a breath. "He's gone."

Also by Mary Frame

Imperfect Series:

Book One: Imperfect Chemistry

Book Two: Imperfectly Criminal

Book Three: Practically Imperfect

Book Four: Picture Imperfect

Book Five: Imperfect Strangers

Book Six: Imperfectly Delicious

The Dorky Duet (Plus a companion novel!)

Ridorkulous

Geektastic

Nerdelicious

Time after Time Series:

Time of My Life

If I Could Turn Back Time

Castle Cove Mystery Series

Fake It to the Limit

Too Much Crime on My Hands

You're the Con That I Want

Fox Family Series

Between a Fox and a Hard Place

The Fox and the Rebound

Another Fox Bites the Dust

Some Like It Fox

For Fox Sake

About the Author

Go here to sign up for the newsletter!
www.authormaryframe.com
Mary Frame is a full time mother and wife with a full time job. She has no idea how she manages to write novels, but it probably helps that she's a dedicated introvert. She doesn't enjoy writing about herself in third person, but she does enjoy reading, writing, dancing, and damaging the ear drums of her co-workers when she randomly decides to sing to them. She lives in Reno, Nevada with her husband, two children, and a border collie named Stella.
She LOVES hearing from readers and will not only respond but likely begin stalking them while tossing out hearts and flowers and rainbows! If that doesn't creep you out, e-mail her at:
maryframeauthor@gmail.com

www.ingramcontent.com/pod-product-compliance
Lightning Source LLC
Chambersburg PA
CBHW020417260626
47156CB00007B/2429